UNREAL CITY

Michael Smith is a writer, fi   ᴧer and broadcaster. He is the author of two works of fiction, *The Giro Playboy* and *Shorty Loves Wing Wong*, and has written features for the *Guardian*, the *Observer*, the *Idler* and *Dazed and Confused*, among others. He has made a number of short films for BBC2's *The Culture Show*. His short film *Lost in London* was premiered at the Barbican Centre, London, in June 2012.

by the same author

The Giro Playboy
Shorty Loves Wing Wong

Unreal City

MICHAEL SMITH

Foreword by Andrew Weatherall

FABER & FABER

First published in 2013
by Faber and Faber Limited
Bloomsbury House, 74–77 Great Russell Street
London WC1B 3DA
This paperback edition first published 2014

Typeset by Faber and Faber
Printed in England by CPI Group (UK) Ltd, Croydon, CR0 4YY

A CIP record for this book
is available from the British Library

ISBN 978–0–571–23581–0

2 4 6 8 10 9 7 5 3 1

The Deep Hum (at the Heart of It All)

Michael Smith was not an attendee of R. D. Laing's 'Anti-University of London', situated in Hoxton's Rivington Street in 1968. He did not buy Post-New Romantic kecks from Willie Brown's Post-New Romantic kecks shop situated in Hoxton's Charlotte Road in 1982. As far as Soho's concerned, he was never called 'Cunty' by Muriel Belcher* on entering the Colony Rooms and never settled Julian MacLaren-Ross's bar tab at the Highlander. He never shared a snifter at the Gargoyle with Nina Hamnett. He is, however, part of a recent history of the demi-monde that frequented (and in some cases still frequents) Hoxton and Soho. He has witnessed the gentrification and franchise sanitation of two personal bohemias.

There are two ways to deal with the loss of a personal bohemia. The first, easiest and most soporific is nostalgia: a vision of a probably non-existent Arcadia with all hardship and regret expunged. In some this is fuelled by an

* On reflection, I think Mr Smith has been on the receiving end of this colourful sobriquet.

envy of the young. Nostalgia is one of humanity's default settings, and has been for countless generations. I would imagine the original denizens of sixteenth-century Soho (though it was admittedly not known by that name until some years later) complained that the sport (in their case hunting) was not what it had been, just as the denizens of sixties Soho bemoaned the fact that the sport (in their case characters and carousing) was not what it had been. And so on, and so forth. Paradoxically, although nostalgia can be mentally debilitating for its practitioners, it is also part of what attracts the next generation of demi-monde to a particular locale. A demi-monde that brings an area to life and, more often than not, eventually brings property developers to the area.

The second way is the path of wistful resignation with a homeopathic droplet of cynicism. This is Michael's Smith's way. This is the way of *Unreal City*. Metaphorical battlefields are revisited and old skirmishes are put into context when Michael is drawn back to London after a seaside sabbatical; drawn back by the irresistible hypnotic hum of the metropolis. All great cities resonate, and it is to this exquisitely dangerous frequency that the true flâneur will always be tuned. Michael Smith's London is still rich in fable, cloaked not in a hankering for an unattainable past, but rather wrapped in self-awareness. An awareness that he is a small part of the perceived problem, and that nostalgia is not only an attempt to drown out inner guilty voices – it can also drown out the sound of the hum: what

Michael describes as 'the deep hum at the heart of it all'. An awareness that, as Joe Kerr puts it in the Introduction to *London: From Punk to Blair*, 'The London of today is the authentic city of other people's perceptions and ambitions.' An awareness that leaves Michael Smith proud to have served, but anxious to embrace new sensations, to be part of as yet unwritten histories. A realisation that fuels the truly exciting musician, artist, writer in his or her search for new pastures to churn into battlefields. A realisation that drives Michael Smith.

Andrew Weatherall

I

ESTUARY EMBERS

Estuary Embers

When the sun gets low above the estuary, glowing against the fishermen's huts and the flat walls of the winding alleys, and the same hazy glow lingers round the Isle of Sheppey in the distance, I'm caught with a strange and familiar sensation of wishing that I could be in all of these places at once, that I could know them all, like this late syrupy sun knows them all, that I could dissolve into its sweet golden gaze . . .

I think about this, wending down those alleys to the chippy, then gazing out across the water eating my fish supper in its paper. I digest the thought slowly, while the sun burns itself out across a lovely red western horizon, lingering in pools that glow like embers across the dark silty spread of the mudflats . . .

Walking along the shoreline, the room above the tennis courts full of stoner kids rehearsing their Floydy tunes, wah wah guitars and jazzy drums floating out of the window, which is open to the sea and the balmy evening breeze, the best rehearsal room in the world . . . past the weatherboarded white pub stuck out on its own on the beach, with old white-haired ponytailed geezers and Floyd proper on the jukebox . . . there's just something about seaside towns and stoners, I guess . . . all the work-aday problems you circle round and round, that blinker you and bind you to your worries and routines are slowly shed, out here before the wide open sky, the magnificent distance of the far horizon . . .

Beyond the ramshackle fishermen's cottages, half a million quid in their battered, black-tarred weatherboard, every Londoner's wank fantasy of a seaside escape, is the real working harbour, where I always end up having a sit and a stare: an ugly corrugated iron silo, sheds, bright yellow diggers piling into huge mounds of grit and gravel waiting to be shipped off somewhere else. . . it is here, sitting in my own secret quiet spot on the dock, staring at these piles of aggregates, that my soul finally finds its rest, poised between a man's need for bloke stuff and the memories of the child and the moody adolescent who is father to the man; this industrial dock is the essence of my early memories, growing up as I did in a dirty northern port, round the corner from corrugated sheds and piles of aggregates just like these, which I would wander round as a teenager, spending long, lonely walks searching for myself, whoever that is . . .

The seagulls sitting on the mounds of gravel have given me back the place I grew up in; though where I grew up is four hundred miles away, whipped by the cold winds of the North Sea, it is the same place: the sun sets behind the same bend in the bay, above the same mysterious twinkling pinprick lights . . . you still yearn to know what life is producing those pinpricks; the atmosphere of seascape and shoreline haunts you, just the same.

The navy blue sea tractor with the wheels bigger and wider than me reverses, with its bright orange lifeboat on the trailer, the whole ensemble the basic block colours of a lifesize Playmobil toy; its amber light flashes round and round, illuminating specks of spitting rain, and I wander on into the violet hour, alone with my thoughts and the vast sky, the lights of unknown Essex towns twinkling along the far horizon, my thoughts turning to hot chocolate and the candlelit cosiness of the hut.

The Hut

You are always woken up by the early morning light and the ping of golf balls from the course behind the hut, the retirees rising early and filling up their days with the calmer pleasures . . . the first half-hour after waking up follows a familiar ritual: set a coffee pot up on the stove, hook the doors open, fold out a beach chair and survey the sea and sky. The strange thing about this seascape is it looks equally fascinating in good or bad weather, and all the weather in between. It's often in between, never quite making its mind up, and I can lose whole days watching the changes of the sky and sea, the many moodswings of this temperamental estuary god . . .

I say good morning to my lesbian neighbours. Half of them are lesbians on my stretch: the seaside is a site of sexual liberty, just as it always has been. It was also the site of the first flush of romance between me and my ex – this little bit of coast is part of us and our story, it played the role of midwife in our early romance. She brought me to another hut a few doors down on date number three; there were storms all weekend, and you couldn't go outside without getting drenched; we didn't, all weekend, and it was heaven . . . when I told this story to my granny she chuckled with a cheeky glint in her eye and said, 'Aah, memories! Eh, son?'

When we went halves on our own hut two months later, it was the grand romantic gesture: a second home before we'd even lived together in a first. I'd bought my half when I was flush, overreaching myself as you always do when the flush of love and the flush of cash coincide, swept up in the heady mix of the two . . .

And now that the girl is gone, the cash is spent, I'm homeless and can't even afford to rent a new flat, I still cling on stubbornly to this beach hut, a grand romantic gesture of another kind: I dream of eking out the end of this long, lean summer here, living on Weetabix and digestives, with five quid fish'n'chips as my treat; dangling a line off the dock wall at high tide and waiting for a crab, taking him home in my bucket, cooking him on the Campingaz stove, cracking him open and eating him – one of the sea's great bounteous luxuries for nowt; in this way, beach hut life transforms poverty into something glorious: the hut was the glory of my flush, flashy times, and now it's the glory of my poverty.

I have no electricity: the emails remain unread, the mobile phone stays off. Candlelight is fine. The sea's as good a bath as any. I like to imagine I'm thick in the heart of this solitude, like Thoreau thick in the heart of his forest, far from the entrapments of modern society, but this of course isn't true – I'm a ten-minute walk from the Co-op, which I can stroll up to for fresh supplies of millionaire shortbread or raspberry pop. I'm five minutes from the Old Neptune pub, where I can sup a Guinness watching some gnarly old Kentish blues band. But still, amongst these modest comforts, the effect is the same: I'm alone, with the space to find a kind of peace for myself, which is also where the words come.

I lived a solitary seaside existence marked by poverty once before, when I was young, and lost, and didn't know what to do . . . this time round is markedly different in one important respect: the wind howls, the walls creak like they might cave in, the candlelight flickers, I write all this down, and I am happy. I thank my lucky stars for this seaside escape – the lucky stars that line up in the vast, sprawling estuarine sky and stand guard above my tiny weather-beaten hut.

Big Belly

I made my way down to the beach in my shorts, ready for my morning swim; I didn't have a shirt on, and a line of special-needs people were walking by on an outing; a short, dumpy black girl with jam-jar glasses on walked by me, looked up and smiled; I smiled back; then she patted my big, fat, hairy belly, laughed and walked off; I chuckled in surprise, and a minute later I patted it myself, with a mixture of disdain and odd satisfaction: I must've spent twenty grand getting it that plumped up over the last few years, and it showed . . .

Going through money as if it were a consensual hallucination, a giddy whirl of lobsters and espresso Martinis, living on a promise that no one ever made me, and consequently no one ever kept . . . the late nights, the taxis back from dirty Dean Street in Soho, passing out at half four in the morning, then waking up hungover at midday – out here, all that seems like a different lifetime ago . . .

I go to sleep when it gets dark, and I'm woken when it gets light again; the toilet is yesterday's milk carton, which gradually fills up with deep dirty yellow behind the frosted plastic, and twice a day I empty it over the fence of the golf course out the back; I wash the dishes in a Tupperware bucket before the open blue sky, and it takes on the air of a sacred cleansing ritual; for bathing, there's the sea; the theme here is a cosmic one – man and universe – and there's very little scope for anything in between.

When I was young and on the dole we used to get our fortnight's cheque and joke we were giro playboys for the day, buying a bag of skunk and turning on the extra bar on the fire, and then being stony broke the rest of the fortnight . . . and now I'm still living like a giro playboy, only older, and the extremes are more so, one minute splashing out on a beach hut and the next minute having to move into it; I'd been living in my own speculative bubble and now I was living through my own credit crunch. Don't ask me what I do. I'm not even sure I know. I'm one of those arty London types, locked in the heroic struggle with lack of work and lack of talent, trying to eke out the lean stretch between now and what's telescoping out beyond the horizon . . .

Dark Waters

The sky was in a strange mood one morning . . . patches of hot sunlight struck the hut, then disappeared again; the sea was a brilliant emerald, then the bleakest, blackest grey, then a shimmering aluminium blue . . . always that morning, the water was restless and changing . . .

This water-place, not quite Thames and not quite sea, has a name, the Nore. Bizarre structures litter it: two huge green and red lights that flash alternately at its edges, giant traffic lights at sea, sleeplessly regulating one of the busiest shipping channels on earth; WWII seaforts, big gun towers on stilts like strange clusters of giant iron mushrooms out to sea; a windfarm sitting in a huge grid, its white turbines turning in graceful synchronisation in the middle of the water; ships so huge and strange, that move so imperceptibly slowly, that when I first saw them I mistook them for Blade Runner fortress-cities, echoes from a future civilisation troubling the horizon; and finally, the beheaded remains of a pleasure pier, a pipe dream of the Raj, a faded oriental Regency crown stranded out there, its neck long washed away by storms . . . the thing that strikes you is how unnatural this watery horizon is: even when she has run out of land, the Great Wen extends her grip; London has such a fierce hold on these waters that even her adjoining seascape is man-made . . .

I walked away from the Nore, inland, up into the wilds of the estuary, an enchanted waste stretching along the shore all the way to the horizon . . . I saw no one for two hours, except two berks with metal detectors in a field, digging for gold, like me I suppose; and also two lads with fishing rods, them angling for fish, me angling for some idea, any idea, about what to do next with my life . . . a certain cast of man is drawn to these empty wastes, pulled in through some deep, obscure instinct, each of us making up our various excuses to come, but coming, really, for reasons that will always remain unknown to us . . .

I ambled up there for hours, until the shadows got long . . . the indescribable beauty of golden hour on the estuary, the mysterious and exquisite feelings it evokes; the tide goes out, birds seem to walk on the water, the sea and land melting into each other, caught in the same glow as the luminous azure sky; strange chunks of concrete rubble, old defences fallen back into the sea; a high tidemark of innumerable bone-white cockleshells; the charcoal-black skeletal remains of piers like rotted wooden ribcages or bad blackened teeth peek out of the water, clustered together like neolithic earthworks, Shorehenge; these water-lands are wastelands, the ruins of our own civilisation . . .

Back at the hut, I contemplated my Ordnance Survey map in dusk candlelight . . . the names suggested it: Foulness, Stoneness, Rainham, Gravesend; the names in smaller print seem to shadow it closer: Graveny Marsh, Shivering Sands, Roach Creek . . . names that stalk the primordial darkness that haunts the river, that permeates this landscape like a mildew, a damp that gets into the joints, the very bones of the place . . . 'Thames' meant 'Dark Waters' in the old language: the dark ancient artery of a dark and ancient empire; dark majestic river god whose race once ruled the earth. 'The Thames has known everything,' said Rudyard Kipling: watery wildernesses, bleak container ports, windswept Edwardian seaside piers; dark waters all the way back to the Tower of London, gothic, gargoyled, all the way upstream . . .

Boarding Up

I woke one morning to a freezing cold beach hut and a filthy, sullen, hungover winter sky. My Indian summer by the sea was over.

After spending the day pottering and preparing the hut, I screwed the wooden boards back on the windows and padlocked the doors, said goodbye to my bolthole, leaving it to weather the winter storms, a time capsule, undisturbed and dusty, till the sun came back again next spring...

My life, and therefore my possessions, had been distilled down to what was immediately essential, downsizing my snailshell from a flat to a travel bag, the rest of it gathering dust in my mam's garage.

I picked up the bag from the decking, looking inland, following the electricity pylons marching off to a smokestacked horizon. A train rumbled past along the same vector of communication and joined-upness, all the way back to the great scabby tit of mother London this Kentish suckling depends upon. I wondered what fist of fun awaited me in The Smoke.

THE BELLS OF SHOREDITCH

Jonah and the Whale

Racing through the sunken soggy marshlands, stalking the vast, dark flow of the Thames . . . London looms like some red giant, firing up the horizon beyond the black emptiness, pulling us in with its monstrous, inevitable gravity . . . falling back through space towards our world . . .

A mixture of apprehension and excitement in the pit of my stomach as the train shears past floodlit oil refineries and distribution depots, the 24/7, 360° radiation of tankers, freight, white vans, an explosion of flyovers and sliproads, the greedy tentacles of the Leviathan grappling up the estuary for food; and further upriver, faraway across the void, fleeting glimpses of the blinking pyramid of Canary Wharf, watching, governing space: a future estuarine civilisation emerging, overlain above the gaps and the wastes of the old . . .

The strangeness of re-entry, the outer atmosphere strewn with neon satellites, multiplex cinemas and TGI Fridays, a fluid night city made of lights, denser and denser, deeper into the city, towards the grinding crush of the centre . . .

Emerging at the building site behind St Pancras, a building site the size of a small town . . . the messy bit behind the West End like the messy wires round the back of the telly, an armageddon of cranes, cement silos, portacabins, yellow flashing lights on diggers, an army of hi-viz Eastern Europeans, the last aftershock of the boom years, the smooth bleached concrete of the new sliproads and bridges all so slick and clean-looking it looks like an architect's model, a computer simulation of the utopia that's now so clearly not around the corner, the future that isn't pulling onto the platform anymore, a wafer-thin glass-and-chrome platform looking every bit like a house of cards against the gothic solidity of St Pancras's clocktower . . . the excitement and apprehension spikes as we dock; it is thrilling to live in what feels like the end times . . .

Stepping off the train, alighting onto London ground, instantly feeling the background city zing, like the zing in the air before a summer storm . . . the intensity, the exoticness, the absolute indifference of the swell of disparate humanity: Polish accents, African eyes, a troupe in sporrans and kilts; the announcements – first in firm, manly English, then repeated in voluptuous female French – produce a delicious frisson, the continental energies radiating out from the Eurostar arrivals door, waves of humanity streaming out with their wheelie bags, tall Nubians with fake Louis Vuitton luggage and leopard-print Cavalli, portly Belgian gents with David Hockney-style architects' glasses, gorgeous young Parisiennes with café-crème complexions . . . London, monstrous wonderland, the city I gave myself to, that gave me back a lifetime in return, the place that had adopted me and many other waifs and strays, now somehow become strange . . .

Strolling through this wide sweep, gazing across the fleet of trains bound for Paris or Brussels, the powder-blue steel vaulting soaring above them, the inside of a giant whale's ribcage, a hymn to the infrastructure of our hyper-connected age; like Jonah swallowed up by it all, by the hum of the giant extractor fans, the deep hum at the heart of it all – back here, home again, lost in London . . .

Babel

London stuns you on re-entry: out into the traffic, an advert with a huge gay arse in it taking up an entire side of the bus . . . a couple overtook me, a chubby black bloke and a thin olive-skinned girl with long, dark hair; I looked at the back of that thick dark mane, catching snippets of a conversation in a French accent about going back to Paris; a moustachioed man on a Victorian penny-farthing wobbled up the street the other way; as they passed each other, she turned to look at him, and then at me – and instead of a French face, I was surprised to catch the glance of an idol of Angkor Wat, the beautiful almond eyes of a Balinese dancer . . . I suddenly remembered why a seaside town surrounded by people just like me could never be enough . . .

Jumping on the bus, up the stairs to the top deck; I couldn't help listening to the Italian in front of me, shouting in a language I couldn't understand: 'Pronto,' he said, gesticulating melodramatically with his Italian hands, to another Italian who couldn't see him, who was probably doing the same thing on a mobile phone in Parma or Turin . . .

I remembered when I first arrived in London, and all humanity seemed to be squeezed onto these Towers of Babel, the great democratic human experiment of the Number 8 from the Bethnal Green Road to Victoria . . .

There were still blitzed-out, roofless old sweatshops I would peer over as the Number 8 cornered Bishopsgate, the goods yard at the crossroads a huge, hollow, derelict hulk in a district full of dilapidated ugly shells, pavement markets full of junk scattered up the streets towards an empty, silent Spitalfields, a loading depot for wholesale fruit and veg that may as well have had tumbleweed blowing through it . . . and beyond this deadzone, the NatWest Tower was a single, solitary skyscraper on the City skyline, back then in the fag-end of John Major's long Tory hangover, before the Gherkin, before the Beckhams, before the Burberry check . . .

You could still smoke cigarettes on buses in those days, there were brass ashtrays by the lovely art deco seats, the Bangladeshi conductor shouting 'Ding-ding! Ding-ding!' at the top of his voice as he pirouetted dementedly up the spiral staircase, who I always looked away from and hardly ever paid . . .

And now, fifteen years later, I still barged my way to the front seat of the double-decker if I could; gliding back into Shoreditch and its knot of boutiquified sweatshops, past the back of a done-up office block I once lived in, where we dropped pizza and spilled beer and got carpet burns from shagging on that rough grey acrylic office carpet, floating above the drunken streets where London had opened her legs for me, gazing out across the streets of my life . . .

Archaeology

Two twins sucking on a she-wolf's tit; I came, I saw, I conquered; people, cities, nations – we all require our origin myths. Mine involves arriving alone in London, setting out hungry from a rabbit hutch, trying to survive on £47.50 a week.

This is my origin myth, and I find a cosy comfort in its exaggerated sense of hardship. These days, I especially enjoy riding past that old block, and looking into the sad anonymous windows from the top of the double-decker, imagining the stories like mine behind them. But riding past it that evening, the brutalist concrete block I first called home had been razed to the ground, and a bird's eye view of a gaping great cavity waiting for construction to begin stood there instead, a toothache-shaped hole in the middle of my memories, boarded off behind computer simulations of happy people in inclusive sandblasted piazzas. I've been here long enough now it's no longer the city I remember any more. The 21st century's scrubbing London so clean the patterns in the underglaze are nearly coming off.

Getting off the bus in the old neighbourhood, setting foot on its streets, it all came flooding back to me: a sweet-tooth's mouthful of toothache-shaped holes in the London of my nostalgia, the London I first fell in love with: all those wildflowers that once poked up through the derelict brickwork, the strange rare flowers of the tarmac wilderness that were the secret life of the city, all tidied up and weeded now, tidied up and gone . . . anyone remember Gary's Bar, which was actually Gary's flat, above the Alcoholics Anonymous office, where you rang the buzzer and got in his lift with 'Please don't disturb the neighbours' written in biro on a bit of paper? Anyone remember The Conqueror, that candlelit locky-in behind Shoreditch Church where you knocked on the door and were answered by the six-foot black lady in the full length leather dress which always smelt of Dettol? Anyone remember the Needle and Spoon?

The Needle and Spoon

Just so I knew it was still there, I made a detour towards my old local, one of the last stubborn understains of the Shoreditch I first fell in love with, the old front line where the Square Mile hit the East End, a high-energy collision that had briefly produced all kinds of short-lived and exotic particles that scattered in intricate spirals through the warehouse canyons, now decayed into a half-life of concept hairdressers and style bars . . . I walked into the dingy warmth of the Needle and Spoon, smiled at the pale skinny bar staff with the pinned-out eyes, waved at Clara DJ'ing, who waved back at me from the turntables with a big smile and a pot on her arm . . .

I only meant to have a cheeky Guinness or two. I ended up staying out all night . . . the drinks were drunk, the sun eventually came up again, nose-ups marking the passage of time, ending up in a wasteground-turned-carpark next morning . . . the folks at my old local had turned it into a jumble sale, making something fun out of an ugly nothing, just like when they used to put on their bank holiday extravaganzas and we'd all get dressed up as Cowboys and

Indians, and they'd cover the floor of the boozer in real grassy turf, or when they used to hold debates over burning questions like 'IS GOD A CUNT?', and a straw poll would be taken at the end and it would be revealed that God wasn't a cunt by the narrow margin of 55% . . .

Julie's carpark jumble sale, complete with pathetic five-foot-long toddlers' paddling pool and a DJ knocking out the deepest, purest disco and Chicago house trax, the DJ who when I went to the bogs to powder my nose again turned out to be a 12-year-old boy, son of one of the pub people . . . and sitting round drinking, gradually decomposing like an avocado in a plastic chair, I had the greatest day amongst those grotty old warehouses, like the good old days were back again and had never gone away . . .

But sooner or later the drugs ran out and it all had to end . . . as I stumbled through the streets I thought about all those good times gone for ever, all those locky-ins and lost weekends on the razzle dazzle, and me being young and up for it gone with them; 48-hour piss-ups, too drunk to stumble home any more, tumbling out of the all-night gay bar into the impossible kaleidoscope bloom of the Sunday flower market, half ten in the morning, the daytime home-builders looking on in bemused horror, and none of it mattering anyway, because all I had to do was get my head down, roll out of bed tomorrow afternoon, go back to work at the bar and do it all over again . . . I suppose that was all any of us were doing, floaters working in bars, just a load of skinny boys in bands and mascara-eyed art college girls living for the weekend and just about paying the rent . . .

The thing was, though, that was then; I was into the wrong half of my thirties now – halfway through my life, if I was lucky – and the last thing I wanted was to be some sad old caner who didn't know the moment had passed, some sad cunt with a Stone Roses hairdo going grey at the sides . . . and anyway, most of the people I knew were gone, dispersed, getting proper jobs and knuckling down, popping babies out and whatever else it is people do, and I knew that if I went back, it was to a new set of barmen and weekenders who didn't look like me any more – they looked far too young and their clothes and haircuts were even more stupid than ours had been . . .

Fashion Street

The sofa I was calling home was in a dingy, windowless photography studio out the back of the 24-hour bagel shop, next to E1's last car lot wasteground, earmarked for a big bastard skyscraper, until the arse fell out of the global economy – the last patch of the ramshackle old City Fringe, living on borrowed time, mercifully spared a few more years. I emerged from the cave-like room hungover at lunchtime, like Dracula in the midday sun. I hardly recognised the terrain any more.

When I first lived on the City Fringe it was all wasteland, all wonderful potential. Nothing above ground but a few fresh, early shoots – a mad pub or two, a few concrete-style bars as austere as cold war bunkers – no cashpoints, no Sainsbury's Locals, no food beyond Pot Noodles from the 24-hour garage – a derelict, clapped-out industrial badland seeping with the mythology of Jack the Ripper and the Krays.

What it did have in spades was art. I remember the first time I stumbled on the place, largely by fluke, coming to an artists' fête: the big industrial French windows of the warehouses that are now occupied by design and PR firms were opened up to ramshackle studios with artists dangling their feet from the first or second floors, displaying their wares, studios full of canvasses, paintings of 'My Boyfriend's Arse' on sale for £20, Tracy Emin staggering around hammered, making an exhibition of herself outside the pub, a pub paved in real grass for the event . . .

Holy Shit, I thought. *This is it, I've found my place in the world . . . I've got to get a piece of this . . .* I'd just left college and was dreaming of spending the rest of my life painting, as many clueless 20-year-olds who've just finished an arts degree do . . . for weeks I wandered canyons of semi-dilapidated tumbledown warehouses with no roofs . . . it was like I'd stumbled across my paradise, my bohemian rhapsody . . .

The once dilapidated warehouses are now covered with expensive corporate graffiti: a mid-thirties hip-hop graf bloke called Ollie or Ben or whatever spray-canning a post-industrial wall, all three storeys of it, standing on a cherry-picker crane thing as bright yellow as a Bob the Builder toy, the kind used by Boeing or British Aerospace, all paid for by Converse or Nike. Half of the inner East End is covered in this bullshit corporate graffiti these days, a mutant superbug recolonising the inner city wastes. Shoreditch is where the creative and the corporate collide – it's the growth industry this whole area's based on. I suppose to say it's selling out becomes meaningless in this context, to say it's selling out is missing the interesting bit:

the bit where the blackened brick has been sandblasted and houses conceptual boutiques with four immaculately creased shirts hanging minimally inside, or destination dining hotspots selling artisan offal and trotters, or the colossal members' bar on the corner of Bishopsgate cross-roads, marking the fault line where the lumbering tectonic plates of London's two leading endeavours, commerce and creativity, collided sometime in the nineties, and the tremors and shockwaves have been rippling out across the East End ever since . . .

Far up on the penthouse terrace of that members' bar, there's an infinity pool where airbrushed people drink cocktails; even though I suspect I should hate it, it's hard not to be seduced by the view of the City skyline, the view from Michael Douglas's mirrored sunglasses, a sky-line that rose like a new Dubai from the desert of the derelict East, that rose like the bubbles up the champagne flute of Tony Blair's London, those heady years of my youth . . . my mate who gets me in there jokes they should have a mannequin in a Michael Douglas suit lying face down in the pool – for decoration, like.

But today, here in the wasteground car lot, I looked up at it all, dumbfounded at this new order rising from the rubbish of the old . . . I bumped into Old Tom, my mate the rag'n'bone man who used to drink in the Needle and Spoon until he got barred for shitting himself, putting his hands down his trousers and then into the bowl of pea-nuts on the bar . . . he still has his junk stall in the parking lot behind the studio, still lives in his caravan in this last remaining bomb-cratered backyard in Brick Lane; it's so strange to see him hanging on in here, this scruffy old relic still scratching a living beneath the skyline of the new Shanghai, one of the last of an endangered species, whose natural habitat had shrunk back to this final patch of desolation, like a polar bear whose ice is running out . . .

I popped into the estate agents to see if they had any live/work units. 'The only one I have at the moment is £300 a week,' he said. '£300 a week? You're mental, aren't you?' was about all I could muster . . . 'You probably lived round here when it was cool, didn't you? You seem to be imagining it's still 1999 prices. It's all international bankers now, and with the credit crunch the landlords are etc, etc . . .' by which time I'd stopped listening completely. It appeared I could no longer afford to be alive, certainly if I was alone. I would have to share being alive, maybe even taking it in shifts. I headed back to the sofa in the damp windowless photography studio for forty winks.

Cunts' Corner

It was Saturday. Like some dowser half-consciously feeling for the water, I walked up into the scraggy end of Hoxditch, as it bleeds into Hackney, to meet the canal . . . the mossy-bricked Victorian sweatshops running along its side seemed strangely bucolic . . . the odd little chimney smoking, like the chimneys of crofters' peat stoves . . . the algae had turned the water into a pea-green carpet . . . a flock of birds roosting in the explosion of bushes poking out from the light-industrial cluster of art galleries were almost deafening . . . the gasworks round the curve were warmed by the last embers of a dying broody sun . . . and in that moment Hackney seemed like some post-apocalyptic paradise, the East End after it's all returned to flowers . . .

The foot and cycle traffic got gridlocked round the floating second-hand bookshop, a canal boat moored by the bridge, magically appeared there like some symbol from deep inside the dream life of Hackney's polite liberal classes . . .

Seduced by the floating bookshop like a magpie round the shiny stuff, I made the mistake of cutting up into Broadway Market, or Cunts' Corner as they call it, for a coffee and a croissant . . . starting to feel put out by the huge queues for the stuff next to the old eel and mash shop, I pondered the peculiar economy that's developed here since the turn of the 21st century, developed across the inner East as a whole . . . Broadway Market has an independent art bookshop, a sustainable and overpriced fishmongers, a pub that specialises in Belgian craft beers . . . we seem to believe we can shop our way out of late capitalism, by consuming in a niche that poses as an antidote . . . this contradictory, ambiguous state is kind of how I feel about the whole thing too, seduced and infuriated by it at the same time . . .

My mood bruised as I tried to relax, watching another young arts graduate expertly pouring the marbled frothy patterns on yet another flat white like it was Renaissance marbled paper, feeling vaguely foiled by this smug café . . .

I often find myself sucked in and then immediately repelled by these crowds – by the self-conscious circus moustache types – and if I'm honest, that marginally subtler stripe of twat who look and sound like me: same Converse, same beard, same semi-employed creative industries small talk; by the 'thank you *so* much' to the waitress for passing the fucking sugar from the pretty, posh art women who have it all, who I simultaneously resent and want to fuck; by them, and by the wild, long-haired children tearing about on wooden bikes that would inevitably result from these conflicted desires. Hell is other people like you.

That's why we run away from villages to the big city in the first place.

I sulked off to the old gasworks and murderous alleys round the back, where this stretch retains its peculiarly dark and enchanting quality . . . before the cluster of cliquey boutiques sprang up, when this strip was like a deserted Spaghetti Western set, and tramps gathered round burning bin drums at dusk, when its magnetic charge was altogether more esoteric and mysterious, the gasworks by the mossy-bricked canal always drew me from my wanders like a moth to a flame; this snug in the bosom of London has always haunted me, drawn me in and caused me to linger . . . whatever that mysterious pull was I cannot say, but I'm sure it's the same pull that drew in the sustainable fishmongers and the flat white artisans, and summoned forth floating second-hand bookshops like the dream symbols of gentrification in the meantime . . .

The Ghosts of Old Shoreditch

Sofa surfing through London is like sofa surfing through my memories, sofa surfing through the streets of my life . . .

A bicycle painted all white with a garland of plastic flowers round the handlebars was chained to the church railings; a shaven-headed man crossed carefully at the traffic lights, studiously balancing a crystal ball on his head whilst four lanes of traffic waited impatiently; there were still some contrarians at right angles to modern life haunting this boutiquified slum . . .

Walking behind St Leonard's, patron saint of prisoners and the mentally ill, past the destination bistros, looking in the windows at the Gok Wan types tweeting on their iphones over a salad, it's easy to forget Old Shoreditch, the richness and the wrongness of it, a richness and a wrongness that fed off each other, making each other stronger . . .

The name once said it all. Shore Ditch, the Roman ditch they threw the dead dogs and buckets of shite over, the ditch that all the flotsam trying to get inside the castle walls shored up against, foiled and ruined . . . the Ditch had been my port of entry too, the borderzone all the bull-shitters and piss artists loitered round, people who knew so-and-so, who were going to do this-and-that, big mouths with a million schemes that never quite seemed to amount to anything, chancers squandering all their chances, snowblinded by a blizzard of white powder, yards of sambuca, bars sticky with spilled spirits, every weekend a bank holiday; there was a subtle, lingering malaise across the area to which many people succumbed; there was a touch of the darkness about Shoreditch, and a touch of the darkness about them too.

It's easy to forget the darkness of that demi-monde, the frightening characters, everything always in excess: Shoreditch in those days was the wild frontier, the City Fringe was also the social fringe, the front line; criminals and psychotics boozing it up with nice kids like us who turned up to gawp, bank robbers and rag'n'bone men drinking with aristocratic Austrian homosexuals . . . the closed circuit of bars was like a demented, drug-addled merry-go-round that spun too fast to get off . . . how did they all endure it, those living ghosts of Old Shoreditch? Where are they all now?

3

ONDON

Sustainability Mural

I got an email from a company I'd never heard of one day, asking if I'd like to participate in creating a mural about sustainability behind Hoxton Market. I don't know anything about murals or sustainability, I said, are you sure I'm the bloke you want for this job? Yes, we know your work, they said. We need Innovators to channel the creativity of the Collective, they said. OK, I said. I got to the mirrored door of their offices, bamboozled. I left even more so.

I couldn't work out exactly what the good-looking people in the fashionable, clean-lined office were actually doing in there, or why the office existed. There was certainly stuff going on, and to all extents and purposes it looked cool. But what all the cool stuff in there actually was, what it actually meant, I couldn't decipher, intrigued as I was. I suspect they may have been an advertising agency.

A globally significant trainer brand wanted to tart up a bit of urban wasteland, the woman who was chairing the meeting explained. She was very attractive, but I just couldn't get a grip on the words coming out of her mouth, couldn't assemble them into any meaningful shape at all. It was something about 'Sport × Culture = Energy + Fun', or something. I don't like sport, I said.

She explained how she wanted me to direct the creativity of the Collective on a day out, appropriating the urban environment, re-imagined and re-purposed as an urban gym. Then silence, and her pretty, expectant eyes. *Now I have to say something*, I thought. I realised the table full of young attractive people were hanging on my silence, waiting for something, anything . . . seconds passed like minutes as the sweat formed at my temples, and I blushed uncomfortably in the silent clean white meeting room . . . This isn't really my field, I said, you'll have to let it marinate a little while.

The rest of the meeting kind of limped along the same way. I left completely perplexed. I still have no idea what they wanted to achieve, or why they thought I would be any use in achieving it. I wonder how clear it was to them.

I got an email later saying it was lovely to meet me and asking me if I was definitely ready to commit. Yes, I said, definitely, as soon as you let me know my fee. I'd already asked twice, before and during the meeting, to no reply. I never heard back from them again.

Perpetual Toothache

A sky somewhere between drizzle and torrential downpour kept me stuck indoors for the next couple of weeks,
chained to the emails, racking my brains, throwing all the
shit I could think of at the wall, seeing if some, any, might
stick. I was getting desperate for some work. No one ever
got back. Like Old Tom, it seemed that I was also some
kind of polar bear scratching around an ever-decreasing
chunk of ice.

So this is what a recession feels like, I thought: it feels like not
having the money to go to the dentist to sort out the per-
petual toothache; it feels like the tiny grains of smelly foam
continually wearing away from the inner sole of down-
at-heel shoes under your socks, and no new pair on the
horizon . . .

A recession looks like the studio of the 360° new-media
company you're waiting to hear back from, with its four
desks huddled into the corner of a draughty, deserted,
carpark-sized office block built in the boom, receiving
a steady trickle of increasingly panicked emails from
people like you, and no one in the skeleton-crewed office

replying . . . or if they did get in touch, trying to blag you into doing jobs you can't afford to take, and this situation becoming so normal that working for nowt almost begins to seem reasonable . . .

The wheels of my industry had seized up . . . the creative industries nowadays are like coal mining in the eighties . . . but then I couldn't really complain – arty types had always expected to be poor, there was just this bubble when I was young and impressionable, and thanks to the Gallaghers and that arsehole with the pickled shark we all bought into this false dawn where we imagined we could make a living from being creative.

Now it seemed business was back to normal, back to the breadline, only all London's bohemian garrets had been turned into the boutique front-of-house for some horrible multinational denim corporation, further down the food chain, tarted up into unfathomably cool offices squeezing you till you squeak, blagging you into becoming a free content provider for the whole ungodly exercise . . .

Bank

My bank is dwarfed by the towering financial edifices of the City of London, squeezed in between Lloyds, the Bank of England and the Stock Exchange. It's a tiny socialist bank with hardly any branches. It's the only bank that would have me. On days like today, the conspiracy of circumstances relegating me to the outer wastes of the financial universe also compels me to wander into the singularity at its centre . . .

It's only half an hour's walk from the studio to the crucible of free-market capitalism . . . round the back of the art deco council block, past the litter and the grubby window which is always open to the maddening sound of a man playing the noisy Grand Prix computer game every day instead of going to work, skirting the edges of the fashion catwalk that flows down Brick Lane and deltas off into Shoreditch, a gold lamé river, kids with three haircuts at once, kids with no idea who they are . . .

Crossing Bishopsgate is passing through a membrane into an entirely different order. Breaching the edges of the Square Mile, heavy weather, gloomier forecasts, financial and meteorological; my head hurts, my sinuses ache, I worry about where the next paycheck will come from; a billion financial isobars bear down on this square mile like the leaden anvil of cloud above it; the dead pressure bearing down on everything moulds the jowly physiognomy of these waxy-faced, grey-suited seabed inhabitants, predatory shoals of the murky depths; they should have luminous filaments protruding from their foreheads, to light their way through the subterranean gloom . . .

Even the sound of the place – Lon Don – is a heavy, dull thud . . . Leadenhall, Castle Court, Pope's Head Alley, the winding passages and rat-runs round here induce the feeling of subterranean burrowing, the feeling of these ancient edifices bearing down on you, the feeling of being buried alive . . .

This is the heart of the financial black hole, zero space and infinite gravity, space twisted up so tightly it bends back on itself, and even light can no longer escape this stormy London gloom.

Bank: only a city as mean and greedy as the City of London could call this black hole crush its centre. It's taken me years of wandering past it to realise that's even what it is; but on a map of the Square Mile you can see this fact at a glance – the eye of the storm is the Bank of England – all roads lead to it like the centre of a spiderweb.

Like Nelson over in Trafalgar Square, a statue of Wellington is set at the centre of this crossroads, Lloyds, the

NatWest Tower, the Gherkin, the full force of English capital clustered behind him; and in the middle of them all, like the grille of a Rolls-Royce, the classical temple of the Royal Exchange, bearing the inscription 'The Earth Is the Lord's, and the Fullness Thereof'. The lord . . . I try to imagine what kind of a mad god could be the lord of this labyrinth: the eye in the dollar bill, the eye in the blinking pyramid of Canary Wharf downriver, the totem of some unseen and increasingly jittery and demented hand . . .

I nipped up the unassuming steps of my bank, wedged between all the pomp and splendour like an embarrassed cough, and joined the other unlikelies in the queue . . . I wondered if the lord of this place might be just demented or jittery enough to cut me some slack, offset against this fullness . . . it seemed no less ridiculous than the colossal wrecks around us getting back on track and paying their portions back, my plight in its own maddeningly trivial way the same as the civilisation I found myself sinking with . . .

Water Music

No one was authorised to speak to me in the bank. But they did let me use their phone to ring the debt department in deepest darkest Lancashire. My ethical socialist bank wouldn't help me with my banking problems. They also told me that because I couldn't afford to keep up my loan repayments, they wanted me to pay my overdraft off for good measure. I have thought about this decision many times since, and the logic of it still escapes me. I walked in owing them two and a half grand and came back out having to pay them four, which would turn into five with the extra thousand pounds interest this new figure would generate for them. Twice as much money in the space of a 38-minute phone call. I wondered whether I would get a better deal at a more successful, less ethical bank. At least they would have more branches.

Scratching round the City of London afterwards, the sky as steely as a razor, so at odds with everything I thought I might fall off the edge of the world . . . I passed two City Boy tailors closing down next door to each other, GLOVES £5, HATS £5, SILK TIES £5; hedgefunder's pink shirts and cufflinks on sale in HACKETT, LONDON, but the L from the sign had fallen off, so it said ONDON, and London did feel undone that gloomy grey afternoon . . .

I thought a walk by the river might help. At London Bridge, the sight of the Thames stopped me where I stood. I stared over the edge at the vast brown body of water, churning ceaselessly, a million tonnes of dull metallic river slowly trickled here through the soils of England . . .

I chanced upon some stairs that no one ever uses, a strange stone labyrinth that descends down to the water through the bowels of the bridge, a dingy piss-stinking maze of tight curves down to the mossy green old boatman's steps by the slow, heavy lap, lap of the water, the slow lap that seems like the very soul of this city, stony old London by the Thames . . .

A riverbus pulled up, and the urge grabbed me to alight . . . sailing away from the City, under Tower Bridge, the boundary of a magic circle that encloses its skyline, nestled there inside it like the crown jewels sparkling on the silvery river . . .

And as I stared at the dome of St Paul's, I thought about the word 'RESURGAT' – 'It will rise again' – the motto underneath the sculpture of the phoenix rising from the flames there: Great Fires, Blitzes, financial shitstorms shall not wither her – London as heavy as Henry VIII's armour, London as light as a Savile Row suit, always poised, power restrained, London always ready for it – or at least that's how I hoped it was, strolling round the deck of the Titanic for all I knew, the tiniest cog in a vast machine whose architecture and arc of fate was way beyond my understanding . . .

Canary Wharf loomed into view downriver; what's it winking at? The power behind its pyramids and towers seems far shadier than the strange cargo of its old docks, gunpowder, ivory and slaves . . . following the squiggle in the river, the navel of the financial world, clouds rise at triangular angles off the blinking pyramid – Canary Wharf creates its own weather, just as it creates its own financial storms and cycles . . .

I jumped off the waterbus at Canary Wharf, risen on its water like some mirage of the future . . . I joined the suits beneath the steely majesty of its edifices . . . if money is the god of this place, then the suits are its priestly caste, their abstract financial operations are the esoteric rites of its high unfathomable religion. I watched the FTSE index zoom round the curve of a huge building in amber LEDs. Newscorp was down one point. Anglo-American was down 2.76. I have absolutely no idea what this means. All the arrows pointed down though – it looked bad . . .

I got to the bank of the river, while a final rosy sunburst brought golden glints out on the Thames, while the lights of the Leviathan began twinkling – lights on the Millennium Dome, lights on the City Airport planes coming in downriver, lights on the sugar factory at Silvertown, supertankers bringing big brown mountains of the stuff in to dock from sunnier climes . . . they open up their cargo doors as they drift upstream, and sundown is saturated with the golden smell of molasses, of sweetness and light, and it seems to me that the Thames becomes the Nile, the Ganges, the World River; and on this World River, I swear I can still see the edges of the future poking into the present, can still trace the outlines of an emerging civilisation that will eclipse all previous Londons . . .

4

DIRTY DEAN STREET

Where Nobody Knows Your Name

London taught me the art of getting lost. It only takes one lucky turn away from the well-trodden path, and all of a sudden I'm in a totally unfamiliar city . . . down the kink of a dog-leg street, a chimneysweeps' row behind the buried River Fleet, I stumbled upon the perfect London boozer, an anchor for those souls unmoored and lost in the urban drift . . .

I got lucky with the comfy chair in the corner, and settled in to watch the tapestry of London life weave itself round the bar . . . postmen, fit foreign birds, a shy couple on a date, a cantankerous old eccentric . . . what struck me as I looked on was the colour, the eccentricity of the cross-section: the average Londoner doesn't exist, the man on the Clapham omnibus is a mirage; the London pub is like the feeding pool in the jungle, the place where predators and exotic birds rub shoulders, a stage on which the great social drama of the metropolis can play itself out . . .

And in the centre of the swirl was the barmaid, and I caught in her smile a glimpse of the London Barmaid, a goddess who appears in many forms . . . many times

I've stood at the bar and composed hymns to this brazen, brassy deity in my head . . . she's the prow of the ship, the heroine of the melodrama; she treads the boards of the bar like she treads the boards of London life; that flashing smile that's seen it all, known it all; she knows everyone, has a thousand lonely suitors – rich men, poor men, old men, young men, heroes, villains – but when she flashes you that naughty, dark-eyed, knowing look, you'd swear it was just for you . . .

I lingered over two drinks, taking in the life of the boozer from the background, with the minimum interaction. Sometimes I like to drink at the bar where no one knows your name. The greatest freedom London bestows on you is London lets you be alone. And then I left the pub, happy, and wandered off into the West End . . .

Drifter

A Drifter chocolate bar seemed the appropriate snack for my wendings through the city, like Kendal Mint Cake for a mountain climber . . . chewing a finger, passing over the Fleet, the hidden geological border of the East and West Ends . . . soaking up the strangeness of a Wednesday afternoon on Leather Lane, feeling an atmospheric change, a different terroir, like tasting two great wines from neighbouring vineyards: the East End's dark, brooding mystery, to the West End's elegance and finesse . . . passing into Westminster, a classy, sure hand takes the reins, and the London cacophony begins to follow a conductor, a plan: colonial spires on neoclassical porticos, tree-lined curves in stately Portland stone; grey pigeons, grey suits, graceful stone of this grey and lovely city, this vast fossil record accreted over the generations, layer under layer: London, a city with so many tomorrows, so many waves swelling and then crashing, leaving us shipwrecked in this coral reef of brick and stone . . .

Windowshopping

The West End is one vast sweetshop. Today I was a non-paying customer, a windowshopper lost among its luxuries, looking at bags and cardigans I can't afford, wondering what all these frothy, fat-of-the-land people in nice shoes do, where all their money comes from, and how I could get my slice of the pie . . .

Drawn in by the waft of the perfume shop, a blend of Portuguese herbs commissioned for a Bristol port dynasty . . . I got a touch of the Blenheim Bouquet on my skin, the cologne commissioned by the Duke of Marlborough to celebrate his victory over the French; windowshopping whiffs of England's epic drama on my wrists and shirt . . .

I can fantasise about premier cru clarets from the time of Coco Chanel, I can see the lamp posts of the West End emblazoned with her CC logo, a wink from her lover, the Duke of Westminster . . . a statue of Beau Brummel, the godfather of the Savile Row suit, those radar-proof stealth bomber suits that cost more than your car, with his maxim, 'To be truly elegant, one should not be noticed,' quoted discreetly beneath him, while I discreetly windowshop dreams, history, sensibilities that are not naturally mine . . . the West End drifter consumes shifting atmospheres and ambiences every bit as much as the Westfield shopaholic consumes Jimmy Choo shoes.

Entering Soho, watching it turning its street corners, the choreography of its complex ebbs and flows, wheels within wheels, the crossroads of that city life I left the sticks to discover: restaurant windows full of langoustines and legs of Spanish ham, neon signs for sex upstairs, snippets of conversation – 'Yeah, get a bag of sherbet, I'll pay you later,' says the white-van man; 'So did you miss my charming company?' says the pinstriped strider on his mobile, smoking the strong cigarette – the social zoo, strata overlaid upon strata, colliding here at the crossroads where everything joins up and meets . . .

Lobsters

For me, Soho once serviced every appetite, every need, every desire. It was the crossroads of the metropolis, the meeting of minds: long boozy lunches hatching some improbable plan, then repairing to the French pub for digestifs, bleeding into long sessions with red-nosed thespian pensioners in jaunty panama hats, boozing into the early hours, ending up down the stairs of the cellar bar, the anti-social club, a last-chance saloon for the desperate individualists, doing lines off the toilet with a 75-year-old trumpet-player who used to sell it to Brian Jones, by which point you're more than likely going to end up leaving in the wrong taxi . . .

I remember the first time I ever ate a lobster, on one of those long lunches, some demented rite of passage one rainy November afternoon; I'd had a late one the night before and had only been out of bed an hour and was very drowsy heading down a drizzly Dean Street through the crowds, and then entering a warm, noisy room completely at odds with the day outside; I was handed a flute of champagne the second I walked in, not even having had a coffee or any breakfast yet; the smiles and sparkle of people I liked and admired all gathered together in one room . . .

I remember the sense of occasion sitting down to the big long table; I got caught up in it and decided to push the boat out and ordered said lobster; I'd never eaten one before and it was certainly a sight to behold when it arrived, sawn neatly down the middle and laid in two halves like a Damien Hirst cow sculpture on a bed of rocket; its anatomy laid bare before you, an apocalypse of eyes, brains, intestines, eggs, and all those lovely juicy fleshy bits . . . the sight of it all seemed almost indecent, but I got stuck in anyway; those exquisitely succulent tasty bits in the tail, cold and watery and fresh in that rainy November lunchtime; even the ritualistic equipment they gave me to eat it with was fascinating – I wasn't aware eating a lobster required specialist cutlery: a huge nutcracker-like tool for breaking open the claws and getting at the soft flesh inside; the silver-plated screwdriver thing for gouging out all that muscle from the legs . . .

Then off for big lines of chang in the toilet while the party got madder and more drunk downstairs . . . a little while later I was so drunk and full I had to recline on a chaise longue . . . *how the fuck did I end up here?* I remember thinking to myself as I looked up at the pictures on the walls . . . I felt like an obese Prince Regent in one of the satirical 18th-century cartoons that hung all around me . . . those lunches were certainly something, but I couldn't help feeling that lobsters and champagne can't come for free, and that sooner or later I'd have to pay for it one way or another . . .

I'd been drinking all day by now and had lost any sense of what was socially acceptable: I ripped a writer lady's notepad up because she said something to me that wound me up; my big burly cousins were in town from the boon docks and I invited them down; it didn't even occur to me I wasn't a member or that bringing them into a literary luncheon club frequented by characters from an Evelyn Waugh novel would be a bad idea . . .

It was. I woke up the next day, in my box room, with a vague but cripplingly acute sense of shame, wondering just how much damage we'd caused; then I got the call from M asking me where the hell her bloody antique plank from the stairs was . . . she sounded pretty cross . . . I had no idea where her plank was and couldn't really remember the last few hours of our adventures at all, but I figured one of them two burly bastards must have had something to do with it . . . so I phoned up Our David and he said he was so sorry but he'd just ripped it up out of the floor for a laugh and taken it with him because he wanted to keep it as a souvenir of Soho, but he'd got bored with it pretty quick and thrown it in a skip somewhere off Berwick St. I ranted at him that that was a fine way to fucking behave and told him he'd never drink in Soho again; I wondered to myself whether I would either . . .

Doors

When I first arrived in London, I would wander Soho's streets, staring down at cellar doors, looking up at louchly lit windows, seeing the buzzers of those dodgy doorways leading to hidden rooms full of shady promise, and wonder when those doors would begin to open up for me ... thanks to a hangover, a hostess and a grope, that whole hidden strata of Soho revealed itself one sun-soused boozy afternoon I remember much clearer than yesterday ...

It started with me dozing happily in the dusty morning sunlight, and the warm afterglow of the night before ... I was blissfully content to be snuggled up in my bed after the vague memory of that crazy night ... a buzzer kept buzzing somewhere far off on the edge of my sleepy consciousness ... then I heard the hostess bark, 'Oy! Cunt! Stop ringing my fucking bell!' from the window upstairs and I shot up with a start ... shit, I was still on the banquette in that weird members' bar! It all came back to me in a shameful flood: the champagne, the wood pigeon for dinner, nearly falling out the window, dancing around to the old Dixieland records with the hostess when everyone else had gone, groping at her like a circus bear and then passing out on the bench . . . oh Christ, what would she think of me now? What a prick I was . . . there was still half a bottle of red left on the side . . . I got stuck in . . . the hostess breezed into the bar with a knowing smirk and I bowed my head in shame . . .

'And how are we this morning?' she smiled,

'Oh M, I'm so sorry . . .'

'Nonsense, darling, it was all good fun . . . now, can I get you a Bloody Mary? Christ, did you hear those fucking bailiffs on the buzzer all morning?'

Well, thank god for that . . . all good fun . . . none of it seemed to faze M, a magnificent woman with her dark Persian eyes and curly black locks and singular force of character, swanning around her members' bar like she was treading the boards . . . I felt all foolish and shy now as she told me about our drunken fumble and then me passing out and her putting a tartan rug on top of me and leaving me to sleep it off . . .

We were both very quickly half cut again . . . she decided today would be a good day to go out on the razzle dazzle round the Soho clubs, and it would be her pleasure to pop my cherry in this regard . . . she left the club in the capable hands of the lezzer barmaid and we headed out into the mid-morning streets . . . I had the distinct sensation it was really about one o'clock at night and we were out on the piss round the streets of moonlit Soho, despite the fact it was bathed in crisp morning sunshine and everyone was off to work instead of eating kebabs and pissing down alleys . . .

The first place she took me was up the wonky Georgian stairs of the writers' club, that amazing smell hitting you upon walking in, the smell of proper exquisite London cooking, of rosemary and goose fat and the roast beef of Old England, a smell I always think I catch now when I wander past the alleys and kitchens of Soho . . .

Then there was the big black cellar door that led down into the exquisitely dingy Georgian townhouse with the Hogarth prints on the wall and the roaring wood fire and the side room with the rococo bed in it, where the famous Italian actresses got their kit off one crazy night after the variety show but I got plastered and left too early and missed all the action . . .

There were these doors, but best of all was the seedy green door like the door of a knocking shop, the buzzer that read 'Cunty', leading up to the tiny bottle-green room, a shady, shabby oasis set adrift above the rooftops of Soho, the rooftops like a choppy alcoholic sea outside the dirty window panes; dukes and earls getting drunk with the sons of great train robbers, Damien Hirst spot paintings getting grubby and tobacco-stained on the wall, a Sarah Lucas self portrait made out of cigarettes, ancient photos of Lucian Freud and Jeffery Bernard and Tom Baker in his Doctor Who days plastered at the bar, the glasses and the antique till embossed with the legend 'Cunt', the broken piano that was just about playable, and when D staggered in to meet us later he just about played it, got the old Knees Up Mother Brown going, and we all sang along shitfaced, and M looked like some strange Iranian angel in the smoky, dusty dying light that cut shafts through the dirty window . . .

In magical thinking there's the idea that the name of something somehow distils and crystallises its essence, and in the case of Soho this is true: 'Soho!' was a Norman hunting cry, from the days when William the Conqueror would chase deer in its open pastures . . . it may as well still have been that way for me, and I lost myself in it: too much red wine and too many nights out on the tiles, losing myself up seedy stairs, behind Green Doors, and nights like Cabaret Night . . .

Cabaret Night was exquisitely dingy and so packed with arch-looking Soho types in feather boas and trilbies you hardly had room to smoke a cigarillo . . . a wrinkly old lady singing jazz standards, a Russian pianist singing songs of vodka and death, a man in a blonde wig and pink polka-dot dress with an acoustic guitar singing Buddy Holly covers . . . an evening in that louche little room was like getting arseholed in a bottle-green George Grosz painting of decadent 1920s Berlin . . . The Green Door was without doubt my favourite bar in the world; the only thing wrong with it was that it closed down, and that empty dingy doorway now stands like an ugly gap where the two front teeth in Dean Street's dirty grin used to be . . .

The Home We May Not Have

The Green Door had been shut for about a year. The the next time I saw all that crowd in one place was Michael's funeral. It was the perfect funeral, a celebration, a triumph. If that sounds callous and heartless it isn't. It was entirely fitting for the man who's life's work had been to get Soho hammered, the waxy captain of that queasy green room that creaked and swayed as he navigated it over the choppy alcoholic rooftops of dirty Dean Street. He'd run it for twenty years, inheriting it as the favourite barman of the previous proprietor, whose ashes were in a bronze portrait bust that perpetually scowled from the bar.

The club had been his life and it ended up being his death – he survived it by only a year. I hadn't seen him in that time and had seen little of the members. As I stepped off the Tube at the cemetery stop I felt apprehensive, and decided to stiffen my resolve with a quick one at the Mason's Arms, alone, before the onslaught of old faces. I walked into the bar and a sea of charcoal suits, peopled by every pasty-faced boozer in Soho.

If Shoreditch had been my port of entry, that little green

room was in a circle somewhere closer to the secret heart of it all, a magic circle surrounded by salt, hermetically sealed, impermeable to the weekenders and sightseers, who seek but cannot find . . .

Soho's piss artists were serious, committed to their art. To penetrate the place properly you had to put the hours in: Fridays and Saturdays were 'Amateurs' Night'; the French pub had two sides, the 'Shallow End' and the 'Deep End', the latter being where the old men with knobbly red noses sat and rotted away; the Deep End of The Coach, the Coventry where all the old red-nosed alchies too crazy for the French were sent, was called the 'Hospice'. These old soaks who long ago made a career choice out of boozing – louche, posh, vaguely artistic, piss artists who've been at it all their wasted lives . . . I always felt I'd arrived at Soho's last dance: Soho was slipping into the world of memories, and that summer, into the world of funerals.

I bumped into my friend Robert Rubbish at the bar; we necked a few amarettos, 'to line our stomachs' – it was too early for brandies – before the procession to the crematorium. I met more old faces on the way, saw M, who'd first taken me down to the club, and it made me laugh, to think that passing out on her banquette like a drunken sex pest had introduced me to this whole subterranean strata of London. All that because of a drunken grope. That initial spirit or energy or whatever you'd call it was a seed that contained the entire future drama within it like the DNA of an unfolding flower.

As the crematorium filled up, the tears and mourning mounted. I felt uncomfortable. I didn't know how to feel or what to think. My eyes welled up as the coffin came in, but when I saw Dick, Michael's old right-hand barman shouldering it, walking up the aisle, he had the most impish, mischievous grin on his face, and I knew the meaning of today was a celebration. The priest, a drinker in the club, which he described as 'a kind of alcoholic self-help group', set the tone: 'Michael died at 52, which many would consider an appallingly young age to go; he did, however, drink to excess, smoke to excess, stay up too late, and I doubt that longevity would be high up on his list of ambitions.' The coffin, by Michael's artist friend, was made out of the kind of cardboard you'd find in a skip, bound up with emerald-green gaffer tape. It had two 'This Way Up' arrows in marker pen and a bigger arrow pointing flame-ward. True to form, the coffin was too big to fit in the incinerator. The funeral ended, coffin still on the slab, with the old sign from above the bar lighting up, with the legend 'Step Up, Spend Up, Drink Up and Fuck Off'.

A green Routemaster bus drove the crowd from the cemetery to dirty Dean Street. That sunny afternoon wake on the pavement outside the club was entirely mobbed . . . despite the Italian waiter's protestations, the drunken mob congregated round the old green door, which had now been painted a forgetful magnolia. Marker pens emerged, people began to scrawl their last respects. 'Piss off, this is our door now,' the waiter said to a chorus of laughter. The thing is, it wasn't his door. It belonged to the drinkers of Soho. He may have painted it the blandest magnolia, but to everybody present that door would be forever green.

It was much more than a drinking club, that place. It was, in the words of one graffitied phrase, 'The Home We May Not Have'. By the end of the wake, people's loyalty to the club was verging on the hysterical. People scrambled over the back roof and pulled chips of green paintwork from the dirty old windows like they were bits of the True Cross, like they were bits of the Berlin Wall . . . as the sun went down I remember David Brown with wine-red teeth, drunkenly, triumphantly holding aloft a flake of paintwork in that wonderful wine-bottle green . . .

That singular green was the theme of the funeral: the men dressed in black suits but the women wore black and bottle green: bottle-green nail varnish, bottle-green eyeliner, at one point a Marie Antoinette tit popped out accidentally from the green trim of a black deco dress; a hundred bottle-green balloons let loose outside the shady old doorway to soar up into the baby blue Soho sky . . .

And just before waking up, hungover and happy the next morning, I dreamed of that Dean Street green . . . I dreamed that old doorway was mobbed like it had been the day before, but somebody forced it open, and I woke up to the fading image of all the old crowd rushing the Italian waiters and piling up that murky bottle-green stairway to The Home We May Not Have . . .

5

DREAM CITIES

Central Station

Sometimes London seemed like a city that rained every-day, the coldest, most uncaring bitch; sometimes she seemed like a string of balmy, boozy evenings, pub after pub, do after do, an impossible party thronged to bursting with interesting, sexy people flashing the cash . . .

I'd arrived here as a wide-eyed young lad, and fallen head over heels; like most long-term love affairs, it had ended up a complicated and dysfunctional one, but living with her at the moment was becoming untenable, unbearable: these days I felt tormented, demented by this city that once upon a time I'd fallen so deeply in love with . . .

I had a meeting near St Pancras, for a job I neither wanted nor expected to get; I found myself at my favourite branch of a generic food chain, supposedly for its almond crois-sants, but really for its singular location. I sat on one of the outside tables, spinning out the pleasure of a cup of coffee, facing a noble line of trains arriving or departing for Paris.

It's an island of breathtaking poetry, this café, the outside tables situated as they are, dwarfed by the vast upper platform, underneath the huge gilt Victorian clock, the cathedralesque wrought-iron vaulting in powder blue, the quiet cathedralesque light falling onto the fleet of elegant continental trains.

Since my sister left on one of those trains to live in that rose-tinted city, I have found myself coming and sitting on this terrace from time to time, ordering a coffee and an almond croissant and passing my elevenses watching the Eurostars coming in and going out again, imagining her exciting new world at the other end of the line, maybe wishing myself along that line too, certainly willing myself into a mindset that's elevated beyond the gloomy psychic weather bearing down on London at the moment. Coffee with these trains in view rarely fails to lift me. The situation allows my mind the freedoms and poetry it needs, my train of thought becomes intercontinental instead of revised timetable affected by engineering works.

Thank god London got St Pancras finished in the flashy years before the arse fell out of its emperor's new Burberry check pants. 'Welcome to the Capital of Europe', the future-deco Champagne Bar seemed to proclaim. The Champagne Bar – a memorial to a lost golden age as fizzy and intoxicating, as insubstantial and as fleeting as the froth up the champagne flutes.

St Pancras. A hymn to another failed utopia. As compelling a piece of propaganda to the free-market wonderland of Tony's London as the Moscow underground was to Stalin's Russia.

You can't imagine anything like St Pancras being attempted these days. As I sit and sip the coffee I try to imagine the memorials that will come to mark the current age. I try to imagine a Cameronoid architecture. I try to imagine a Cameronoid champagne bar. I try to imagine myself with my sister, in the city at the other end of the railway track.

A Half-remembered Dream

I was sitting by the big ferry windows, watching us pull into Calais docks at dawn, a panoramic sweep of cranes and harbour walls, the whole scene opening out before me like I was watching it on a widescreen cinema . . . I hadn't slept at all and was reaching the stage where everything seemed like a slightly delirious and disconnected daydream I was watching from afar, the elusive memory of a half-remembered dream . . .

I'd decided to run off to Paris on the £20 Megabus. We'd boarded in the wee small hours, I hadn't managed to sleep, and there I was, some time later, espresso after espresso not even touching the sides . . .

The shock of arrival in the alien city, the grottiness round the station like the grottiness round any big city station, swarthy pickpockets and policemen with machine guns; my sister met me off the coach and walked me away from all that, down the art nouveau steps round the side, to a beautiful spot hidden round the corner, and all of a sudden it changed from the dodgy zone to this beautiful little pocket of laced ironwork bridges and converted warehouses clustered round the canal . . .

We slowed down by the sun-dappled waters . . . the long journey was finally over . . . the sign on the chalkboard of the café said, 'Cette après midi, c'est Chablis', and we agreed . . .

Steam Whistles

Sitting by the sunny water with a glass of wine, I felt for the first time like I'd actually 'arrived' . . . the feeling of being both excited and calm, and at the centre of things; feeling strangely light and still here, with the background frequency of the city charged up all around us, an almost tangible sensation, here in the eye of the storm, and I was strangely at peace within it, watching the play of the shimmering water, the people, the life of the canal, anticipating what might come, the ways in which Paris might unfold for me . . .

Afterwards, we strolled, and what a beautiful sight that canal was, bridge after wrought-iron bridge backing onto art nouveau warehouses . . . at a lock, a boat was waiting to get lowered . . . the skipper blew its whistle to let everybody know, a proper old-time melodic tugboat whistle caused by steam power; and now he had everybody's attention, right on cue the steam whistle started piping out music, like Popeye doing an impromptu set of wonderful French standards like 'La Mer' and 'By the Banks of the Seine' . . . and for an enchanted spell, time hung suspended and everyone round the lock was completely captivated . . . the lock eventually opened, and the skipper took the wheel, this old dude in a neckerchief and cap smoking a pipe, smiling, lapping it all up, the steam whistles still belting the tunes out, while a canalside of delighted Parisians whistled and cheered him on his way, and we went off on ours . . .

Evening East

Twilight in the Marais, sitting at a pavement café, starting off a civilised evening with a long lazy dinner and a bottle of red . . . all the little ways that Paris seduces you: the wink of the waitress, the joined-up spidery handwriting on the chalkboards, the constant flow of chic mysterious people, well-heeled, olive-skinned, sexy and urbane . . . in big cities like Paris the night has a thousand glances, and every single face looks interesting – a thousand singular stories you can only glimpse and guess at . . .

As evening darkened we drifted further east . . . when we passed over the Place de la République, it felt like we'd crossed over some invisible barrier, the familiar Paris was behind us, and in front was the East End, the Paris of the Bastille and the Revolution, of workers and immigrants and grumpy leathery-faced locals who smoked fags that were too strong down to their tarry butts . . .

Heaving streets snaked up hills filled with seedy flea-pit cinemas and Bar-Tabacs . . . the French is spoken with an Arab accent here, they roll the Rs more harshly . . . couscous, kebabs, France's old empire sucked back into its inner cities . . . Cambodian churches, soup kitchens with Stars of David painted on the wall . . . the sense of mixed-upness and collisions, tat shops next to trendy bars, the Paris where life spills out onto the street, where the streets become one big graffitied art gallery, an East End just like ours: the ragged Paris, the restless Paris, the Paris busy be-ing reborn . . .

Bobos

There's a kaleidoscope of Parises which are nothing like the handful that end up on the postcards. Barbès is one, centred on a daunting, monstrous boulevard with oily, screeching art nouveau métro bridges overhead, Senegalese street hawkers trying to con you into buying cheap gold watches, shock-haired nutjobs shuffling along, too many people on crutches. Barbès is the unpretty Paris, the brutal Paris, a pyramid that needs the sweat of slave workers to be built . . .

Clignancourt's another, a shantytown on the edge of the ring road, a dodgy knock-off street market that thrives in the twilight zone of the city's jurisdiction. It looks every bit like the Wild West, or maybe the Ivory Coast, with its one-storey tumbledown shacks and big-arsed African women chewing corncobs.

These are not the Parises most tourists expect, the Parises most tourists avoid, but as a 'bobo', a 'bourgeois-bohemian' as Parisians call them, I'm drawn to the whiff of these marginal zones like a fly round shit.

I have a fantasy of bohemia that cannot be sated by Montmartre or the Latin Quarter, theme parks of Paris's artistic past. But then again, my fantasies of bohemia, and Paris's for that matter, are probably a hundred years out of date – 'bohemian' and 'bourgeois' are two obsolete distinctions that no longer describe the realities of urban society effectively – they're no longer diametrically opposed, but have collapsed into each other in the post-industrial era, where creativity, in the loosest and shallowest sense, is no longer the preserve of a handful of arty weirdos, but is the great growth industry of all the good cities, a yardstick by which they are measured, the industry all the cool people work in, a rapidly multiplying army of worker bees swamping swathe after swathe of the colourful old urban neighbourhoods. All the good bits in the centre of town like Soho or the Marais went through the roof years ago; at this current phase the less lovely industrial inner cities that for some reason always lie to the east are packed to the rafters with bar design consultants, art directors and fashion stylists. I know because I've looked. I search for bohemia and all I find are these bobos. I search for bohemia and all I find is myself.

A Mona Lisa Smile

I decided one morning to go and get lost in the Paris that *is* on the postcards, so I jumped on the nearest métro into the centre . . . there's no smell in the world like the smell of the Paris métro, a warm, dry smell like hot cardboard, inviting you down into the bowels of the city . . .

I got out at the Palais-Royal, walked underneath its long classical stone colonnades; I heard the clinking of glasses and a big round of applause go up from behind one of those elegant long windows two floors above, and having no idea what was going on up there only made it all the more seductive . . .

I walked and walked, deep into this city that gives you so many wonderful opportunities to get lost . . . Paris is one great Mona Lisa smile: passageways and courtyards wink at you, beckoning you to explore them; it unfolds and unravels, layer after layer, always subtler worlds within worlds, unveiled round every corner . . .

And all of a sudden, a change of scale: the city dazzles you on turning a corner, and you chance upon the broad vista of the Seine: you can make out the grand cycle of Paris's evolution, back to its ancient origins, from one end of the river to the other: Eiffel's art nouveau skyscraper and its Chicago-style overhead métros crossing the water on the western horizon, back through the Belle Époque and the Grand Palais dripping with hallucinatory nymphs, past the clean-lined, rational simplicity of the Enlightenment at Invalides, then the royal Renaissance grandeur of the Louvre, and following the bend of the river eastwards, the islands and Notre Dame, Paris's distant fairytale origins rising like a medieval mirage from the water . . .

With shoes touching the wooden slats of the elegant sliver of the Pont des Arts, a bridge that is strangely like an English seaside pier, I passed over from the glass pyramids in the stately heart of Paris to the Académie française on the Left Bank, the guardian of all that refined high French culture, as magnificent and mummified as the Louvre it faces on the other shore . . .

But then I found a discreet little archway hidden in the Academie's side, like the gate to a secret garden: the door to a speakeasy you somehow know the password to, and all of a sudden you move through it into a different Paris entirely, a village hidden behind the grand riverside facades, a rarefied and secret world you can't quite make out behind the doors of the galleries, the exquisitely mysterious hotels, the École des beaux-arts, the little world of St Germain, another wheel within a wheel, and so the adventure continues . . .

The Touristic Romance

Like the song says, everybody hates a tourist – but the tourist, really, is approaching a rare and perfect state. As tourists, cut free from all concerns, corks bobbing along in the great dazzling flow of life, an evening or an afternoon becomes almost unbearably rich, the heart becomes full to bursting, and we find our perfect hours.

The tourist feels a wonderful sensation of lightness, of floating . . . for the tourist, the stranger in the city, everything is experienced at the surface, with only a vague and approximate understanding, and this is actually his blessing – that every passing and vaguely grasped spectacle is full of intrigue and mystery, full of the promise of deeper meanings yet to be revealed; he bobs along the shallows of his strange new city life, enchanted by the shimmering dance of light at the surface, the neon flux of the signs for the cinemas of Montparnasse like moonlight dancing on the shallows, with the unseen depths of the ocean of Paris beneath him . . .

Because I can't understand what it all means, the city is all the richer, all the more resonant and mysterious; because I don't know what Serge is singing about in the songs, my imagination is free to join the dots how it will, free to go off on a kind of flânerie of its own, a flânerie of open-ended poetic association.

Losing yourself in the physical city, but also unfolding before you, the Paris of your interior romantic fantasy, of everyone's romantic fantasy; fantasy and the real world are married here, life and the imagination are locked in a lovers' embrace . . .

Paris Would Be Kinder

I'd escaped from London feeling like either the whole thing was about to collapse, or more likely I was; London seemed cranked up to such unbearable pressure it was eating its own children alive, greedy for the new blood that was always arriving in droves, clotting up the bus queues and bottleneck roads. Or at least that's how it seemed to me.

Paris felt nobler and more humane, felt like she would be kinder . . . from day one and those strolls along the canal, I sensed I had entered into a romance with the city; they say Paris is the most romantic city, and I felt perfectly romantic, alone, without a lady to stroll along the riverbank with: it's a romance with the Seine, a romance with the city itself; and like a sweet and yielding lover, I knew she would be good to me and grant me what I needed . . .

City Life

It was getting near the end of my trip. I lost myself in my sister's local neighbourhood for the day, a little world in itself, a perfect mix of flower shops, butchers, trainer boutiques . . . I didn't need to see the Eiffel Tower or Notre Dame, it was enough for me to potter round this small hidden corner, a neighbourhood lacking any obvious sights, where you don't hear American accents, you hear Parisian accents . . .

I walked through the local park, with the sandy gravel floor, kids running about, teenagers on the concrete table-tennis table, old timers sitting on the lovely green iron benches taking it all in, people playing pétanque . . . and walking around, watching the locals get on with their daily business, an old suspicion returned – that Parisians have cracked the secret of city life, they've mastered the art of living well, like truly civilised human beings . . .

Paris's real promise, throughout its dizzying history of literature, food, boulevards, lingerie, etc, has been exactly this. Though its cutting edge is blunted now, and it's something of a sleeping beauty, people still come here and draw inspiration from its infinitely deep well, get glimpses of life being led more fully and poetically, and take a little bit of it back with them to the four corners of the redneck earth . . .

This is what happened to me as a rucksacked 14-year-old from the back of beyond, gobsmacked, enchanted, in love with a totally new idea: City Life . . . I wandered round Montmartre, perched on its hill like a Euro Disney franchise, like a kid in the thrill and ache of his first crush . . . I lingered at the Bateau-Lavoir, the doss-hole where Picasso invented Cubism . . . I imagined his life there, and Modigliani's, who lived in one of the flea-pit rooms down the corridor, penniless and stoned and cock deep in all kinds of trouble, cock deep in life . . . it crystallised in me the desire for that peculiar life we leave our small towns behind to discover, a life it became my naive dream and ambition to inhabit . . .

Dream Cities

My romance with Paris really flowered a few years later, when I fell in love with a beautiful Parisienne . . . the Bonny Frenchie was a true daughter of her city: her mother had been a can-can dancer at the Moulin Rouge; her dad was one of the waiters. Her first job, aged eight, was picking up the ostrich feathers from the stage after the show. I'm not making this up.

The Paris she showed me was as dream-like as the red neon windmill that turned above the club. Her city always had this dream-like, or maybe story-like quality for me: strolling its sun-dappled slopes and curves was strolling through somebody else's city, somebody else's story, a charmed life I could only understand as a legend, a fantasy . . . the whiteness of every building like the whiteness of the passing clouds, so tender, so elegiac; Paris, the colour of bone; ghostly afternoons in the guts of the city, the ebb and flow of the people going about their daily lives, sleep-walking through the vast mysteries of their city . . .

Paris for me has always been this dream of what cities are, or can be, the place where I first dreamed of that kind of life, all adolescent fantasy and possibility . . . but London was where I looked for that life, and where I found it. When I arrived there as a fresh-faced kid from the boon docks, my initiation into manhood was to go walkabout, alone and skint and surviving on what I could; I lost myself in London, and I found myself in London. I gave myself to London, and London eventually gave herself to me.

6

LOST IN LONDON

Ze Red Brick

Stepping back off the coach into London, oily puddles, dirty concrete and the smell of petrol, I thought about something the Bonny Frenchie's dad once told me, and I smiled, remembering how charmed he'd been by 'ze red brick' that always looked so drab to me, because, obviously, ugly old red brick was quite a novelty for a Parisian . . . 'We 'ate Paris,' I remember him telling me at dinner once, 'ze noise, ze litter, ze hassle – but for you, you don' see it,' and I realised it was quite the same predicament for me and ze red brick of old London . . .

London was some kind of exotic epiphany for him, and just so for the Bonny Frenchie . . . I remember she would barge her way to the front seat of the red double-decker, and as it took the hump of London Bridge and the majestic sweep of the Thames – Westminster, Big Ben, The Eye spread out from one window, the Gherkin, St Paul's and the City from the other – she'd feel a thrill in the pit of her stomach, a thrill that she'd found the special place, the promised land, the navel of the world, like Jerusalem in the minds of the medieval map makers . . .

And coming back here after that bone-white city, ze drab, dreary red brick was transformed for me, and I felt an old flame for London welling up again just like it used to . . .

Fuck Yuo

My friend the Venetian had moved into a big warehouse in the toxic industrial badlands clogging up the banks of the River Lea, a fragile period piece wilting under the regeneration radiating outwards from the Olympics. A futon was available, with windows. I stayed on the bus all the way out East, to the bit where the clamour of nasty Victorian terraces and brutalist highrises gives way to giant chemical drums, corrugated iron sheds and cement works . . .

The Venetian told me to ring him when I arrived, but once I got off the bus, his phone was dead. *Bollocks*, I thought, *I'm trapped in an industrial estate with no directions*. I walked down the road. There was no pavement. The tarmac was a crazy mess of potholes and huge puddles full of strange plastic sheeting. There were industrial-scale bagel factories, mirror manufacturers, warehouses in various shades of dirty brick. No cafés, no shops, nowhere for people to interact; strangely in this ant-hill of ten million people, I couldn't see a single human soul . . .

I walked past an old pub covered in art college stencil graffiti, which I presumed was a squat. I saw some scruffy arty types ride past on their bikes. What were they doing here? As I rounded the corner I walked past a chap with a mackintosh, umbrella and a beard, kind of shabby and dapper at the same time, the way I hope I look . . . we eyed each other up with a mixture of suspicion and regard . . . there was clearly more to this no man's land than met the eye . . .

What did meet the eye was scrubby industrial dereliction to match anything Sheffield or Salford has to offer. And then, suddenly, water! The silty, dirty banks of the River Lea splintering off into myriad streams on the way to meet the Thames at Bow Creek. I couldn't find a way down onto the banks – it was all wire fencing and Alsatians barking at me; plastic bags, detritus, concrete rubble, water forking off everywhere, into canals; how funny the Venetian lives here, I thought, in this anti-Venice: London, New York, Venice, we're all water babies, civilisation is water-borne . . .

I heard the strains of John Lennon's 'Imagine' behind a windowless factory wall . . . a swan glided gracefully past . . . I walked over a wrought-iron bridge and onto a wrong turning . . . on an arid bit of scrubby wasteland I saw my first humans for half an hour – four raggy lads with a pitbull and a quad bike; *Oh, marvellous*, I thought; 'All right lads,' I said, trying to remember I was northern . . . 'All right, mate!' they beamed . . . 'Is this the way to

Fish Island?' I asked, for conversation's sake . . . 'Yeah, it's down that way – do you want a seaty on the back of the quad, mate?' I declined, but felt humble, and a bit guilty I'd presumed they wanted to stab me up . . .

Under a railway arch and down a back alley littered with cans of Tennants and a pissy mattress, the Venetian finally rang, and I headed back up to the graffitied pub, which to my delight was actually a functioning, semi-legitimate boozer serving either cans of Guinness from a bin full of ice or balloons of laughing gas at £1 a pop . . . the room had a squatty we-went-to-art-college vibe, with the appropriate clientele . . . it all made sense to me now: this place was a secret bohemia of sorts; it reminded me of Shoreditch years ago – or, more truthfully, how I imagine Shoreditch was before people like me started turning up.

I loved being around all these cool young artist types: sultry, clever Jewish girls, smiley black girls with afros and silly fluorescent glasses . . . stumbling on this secret little world cheered me up no end, and after a few drinks me and the Venetian began to get very jovial and started mingling. I even did a few bags of laughing gas, went blind and weird for a little bit, like I was stepping back from myself somewhere and observing the consciousness function of my own mind breaking down; when I came to and the ringing in my ears had stopped, I found myself chatting to a cute 25-year-old-Swedish blonde.

I was kicked out of her flat early Monday morning,

exhausted, hungover, elated. As soon as her front door shut, it struck me, like the punchline of a delightful joke: I didn't have the foggiest idea where I was. We were a fair walk from the pub and the Venetian's new place, and ambling back there through unknown swathes of whichever part of Hackney I was in, watching it wake up to another week, the seagulls squawking, the morning sun laying flat colours on the scruffy buildings, it looked like some shoddy convalescent seaside town. It looked gorgeous. I was seeing it through the eyes of a convalescent that sweet Monday morning. Hackney seemed like some dysfunctional village idyll, a messed-up Camberwick Green: the dreadlocked street cleaner beamed and said 'Good morning!'; the Turkish man in the 99p plastic bucket shop said 'Hello!'; the graffiti on the pavement said 'FUCK YUO!' . . . the next thing I came across on the pavement was a single crimson high heel lying next to a bin. This place was either really dodgy or the kids of Hackney clearly have as much fun every Sunday night as I'd just had. Probably both.

Hitting the high street, I walked by the shell of a sweatshop front about to be rebuilt into some painfully fashionable lifestyle unit . . . but before that predictable reality becomes fixed, like this whole area must soon inevitably become fixed, the shell of a building was still all possibility – a shell of light, with dusty early morning shafts beaming through the windows and doors like the sweatshop at the threshold of the pearly gates . . .

And always overtaking me that perfect Monday morning, the young, gorgeous bicycle girls of Hackney, riding to wherever they have to get to, an embarrassment of riches, a traffic jam's worth of gorgeous East End beauties in their red fifties lipstick and their high-up hair in loose sexy twists, Greeks and Norwegians and Persians and Brazilians, their bicycle bells and their Rembrandt swells – a lovely, round, ripe united nations of arses, kneading those saddles like a baker with his dough . . .

DIY

My friend Jo Jo had moved into a terraced house down the road; she'd decided to turn it into an ad hoc restaurant. She invited me and the Venetian round for dinner one Sunday evening, fine dining for forty quid all-in.

We wandered, lost, past the corrugated iron church: an African evangelical church ruining Sunday for everyone else with their terrifying frog-throated preacher who shouted something that sounded like *Hey ba-ba-ba* to whistles and shouts from the congregation in their shiny robes and fancy hats as his tag line grew more and more hysterical . . .

We got to Jo Jo's street, a modest, pokey terrace round the back of a dreary, interminable hospital wall. It didn't seem right at all. I rang the bell on the anonymous pebbledashed house, which looked nothing like a restaurant, utterly confused by now, wondering if we'd got the wrong place . . .

We were ushered in by a glamorous waitress into some kind of enchanted, hermetically sealed reality. They'd stuck about fifteen tables with candles and cloths in the front and back rooms and everyone was drinking and laughing and having a whale of a time in the candlelight. There were five courses, each paired with a different wine, Champagne through Beaujolais, Burgundy and Rhône, ending on a sticky one for dessert, and over the course of my bargain banquet I got very pleasantly drunk . . .

Afterwards, back at the Venetian's factory floor, I stared out of his huge industrial windows for a long time, in love with this secret East I was getting glimpses of . . . you could see a hundred other factory windows lit up in the darkness, and every one of them filled with mannequins, sculptures, paintings . . .

It struck me that these Hackney hinterlands still had a DIY culture – DIY bars with laughing gas and Guinness in a bin, DIY African evangelical churches made out of corrugated metal sheeting, DIY artists' lofts in old factory buildings, DIY restaurants in pokey terraced houses, DIY shopping from the third-world street market, like Hoxditch used to be before it turned into a boutique quarter selling £300 Martin Margiela trousers and organic artisan elderflower cordials . . . and then, as soon as this thought occurred, I saw its inevitable end – an almost finished highrise block of terracotta luxury canalside flats with pine panels, and a huge billboard saying 'The Lock: Live the Lock Lifestyle' in front of a forest of cranes . . .

And I thought about this vast process, about wastelands

and bohemias and impending corporate amnesias, as I gazed across this fragile city of art and its blighted industrial creeks, this anti-Venice that was sinking below the bland, sandblasted infrastructure of the Olympics, while commerce winked from Canary Wharf in the distance . . .

Building Sites

It was Sunday. I did what everyone else does, joining all the other bobos on bicycles, following the posh, pretty art girls past the dodgy cockney lock-ups, the piles of bright yellow skips, an encampment of static mobile homes for Gypsies that freight trains rumble over, across a bridge straddling a ferocious six-lane highway hewn three storeys into the surface of the city, an impassable torrent of traffic rushing down a concrete gorge . . .

And then, on the other side, like the wardrobe that leads into Narnia, I passed through the magic cut, emerging onto a graceful, stately terrace, a neoclassical idyll that articulates the edge of Victoria Park, the slight hiss of the traffic an almost inaudible clue that a different word lies behind the sedate elegance of this wedding-cake stage set . . . one of those cinematic jumpcuts that London is composed of, those disconnects that are a fundamental part of its grammar . . .

I skirted the park, joining the ceaseless human flow along the gentle arc of the canal, the old highway of the Industrial Revolution which is now the highway of the polite army of pedestrians, joggers and cyclists who are quietly de-dilapidating the inner East . . .

Willows wept into the waters . . . daddy coot brought twigs for mummy coot, building her nest on the water; a little further upstream, by the lock, swans the size of Rott-weilers were building a water-nest the size of a kennel, a big round twig kennel with Diamond White bottles tangled up in it; and in the background, cranes and a forest of scaffolding . . . London's a constant building site, like Paris is constantly getting botoxed, or Venice is constantly being propped up – it's a basic feature of reality here, like gravity or the speed of light. Even the coots and the swans are at it.

The weeping willows gave way to the Cold War concrete of the Globe Town Estate, behind Roman Road, a road once known as Drift Street . . . Drift Street, Globe Town, gurgles in a rich river of history, concreted over by Soviet-style highrise, the obsessive-compulsive disorder of sixties functionalism, a clean, forgetful future that never was . . .

And after that came the eco-park, an artificial countryside built on top of factory land at the turn of the millennium, a green amnesia with a dead straight, man-made river running through it, the fragment of a watery garden city utopia like the kind I used to read about in *The Usborne Book of the Future* as a boy, except the Telly Tubby wind turbines never turn and the canal is full of plastic Budgens carrier bags . . . I suppose the future's always fatally shortsighted, always has a child's oversimplicity abut it . . .

And sometimes, cycling through the space and time of this city, I imagine London as a rag'n'bone yard of abandoned utopias . . . a New Jerusalem, a dark satanic mall, sore thumbs poking up through history into the present, while we live in Plan B, cobbled together like a sturdy old boot . . .

The Markets

Shopping for my daily bread, I went for my 'bits' down the local street market, still not overrun by organic delis or people like me . . . I walked by flowers, birthday cards, piles of barbeques in boxes, cheap and nasty Donald Duck bed sheets, the racket of a dancehall reggae stall – still cockney, but with Housing Benefit forms in Bengali, Somali and Vietnamese, like exotic spice on the jellied eels . . . and all the while the eye in the pyramid winked from Canary Wharf, a gaze that governs the global market I find myself a couple of miles from the epicentre of . . .

London is the chaos, the colour and stink of the market . . . from the Stock Exchange to Petticoat Lane selling knock-off Kenwood kettles in its shadow, a patchwork mess of markets scatters and spreads out from the City into the East End – the bric-a-brac of Brick Lane, the flowery bloom of Columbia Road, the big ugly exotic fruits of Bethnal Green – a rich seam of DIY commerce that sews the East End together, an artery bringing all the blood cells and life down along it . . .

London's one big market and always was: in one square

mile I bought cocaine off a 70-year-old Italian barber with a pencil moustache from his shop, a black-cab driver who'd pick you up from one pub and drop you off twenty metres down the road at the next, a fruit and veg market trader who'd give you it in a brown paper bag with a couple of cox apples thrown in for good measure. London society is based on these unlikely human collisions.

I think about this as I say hello to the Bengali corner-shop lady, a nice friendly lady whose name I don't know, whose life I'll never know, whose smile I'm fond of – this pleasant stranger who has been drawn here across vast improbable distances by the magnetic current of the blinking pyramid, the symbol and the centre of the situation both of us find ourselves pulled into . . .

My Secret Lunch

My ex knew how to eat. With her, restaurants overtook boozy nightlife as my skeleton key into the urban pleasures. Our evenings out were an adventure deep into the labyrinthine and ever-changing world of the capital's sophisticated food culture, an infinitely deep well. We split up: I never found out how deep the well went.

Now I'm single, and broke, and can't find any work to fill up the days, I often find myself wandering aimlessly, ambling deep into the guts of the urban inner core of the East; I wander this post-industrial landscape, by canalside factories converted into architectural practices, art galleries and ad agencies, and restaurants mapping the subtly shifting topography of urban gastronomic culture: hi-concept offal, swordfish cicchetti in Campari bars, Catalan tapas on cocktail sticks – which all reminds me, like a kick in the ribs, of the evenings we ate out in them . . .

But if these walks ever take me to the watery canalside borders of Clerkenwell, Hoxton and Islington, I sometimes steal a secret, but not exactly guilty pleasure . . . it's a private pleasure that my ex would disapprove of, that this whole milieu I find myself more and more embedded in would disapprove of: a Happy Meal from the drive-thru McDonalds behind the Texaco garage on the City Road.

The weight of urbane prejudice shames me into keeping secret this pleasure I feel I'm not supposed to enjoy; one time I was at the counter and heard, 'Yeah, a Big Mac meal, lots of ice in the Sprite and plenty of ketchup,' in a familiar gravelly New York voice, and I turned round and saw a notoriously louche art dealer I knew from drinking round Soho . . . we both looked at each other uncomfortably like we'd been rumbled . . . 'Fancy seeing you here,' I said awkwardly . . .

These stolen half-hours are a private pleasure; I like to be left alone. Staff and scrubber mothers no longer eye me with suspicion, since I've realised correct protocol should be to ask for the Happy Meal without the toy, and on a tray instead of the Buzz Lightyear cardboard lunch box.

I find a strange happiness and peace here . . . I feel the last resonance of a redundant and discredited American utopianism I believed in as a little boy; the residual sense of child-like wonder that this simple, primary-coloured environment is designed to exploit; the strangeness of eating on the wooden bench on the tiny manicured lawn by the slow hiss of the sliproad suggesting a toytown suburban anywhere-ness nestled deep in the guts of one of the most knotted-up and historically evocative parts of London, a spectral neo-Grecian obelisk predicting the gothic spike of the Shard it rhymes with, reminding you where you are, beyond the small town amnesia of the adjoining Texaco forecourt...

I finally feel part of the 'real' London here, part of the great majority of its population I never come into contact with – the ginger cockneys in Reebok classics, the rowdy black school kids in the queue, the African women, the Filipino women, the Muslim women in veils behind the tills; we like to pretend we're one big multicultural family in London, peeking out from our flat white ghettos, but we don't actually mix in this city – there are chasms between the different social strata, who know nothing of each other, having virtually no points of contact; McDonalds is the lowest common denominator in a truly democratic sense: it's where the urban melting pot actually happens.

Sitting on the bench with a Happy Meal, quiet and alone and quite content, I am at one with the masses of humanity, the migrations of races to this McDonalds that is all McDonalds, the collective willing towards this universal present tense moment; on this platonic wooden bench, on the universal lawn next to the sliproad, I am everyone, I am you, we are finally all in this together ...

7

CHANCE STREET

Chance Street

Like crossing a street corner and suddenly sensing the changing atmosphere and energies of a different neighbourhood, life in London shifts abruptly, changes with refreshing or saddening regularity, unmoored at every turn . . .

One day I walked into a pub I'd not drunk in for ages . . . the chef, a nice bloke I'd known from years ago, threw me a life raft, in the form of his ex-council flat caught in the limbo before renovation. Being between cheques, I was the perfect tenant-between-tenants . . .

He wanted to do it up and charge extortionate rent for it, but we agreed I'd stay there till he got round to it, so I got a dilapidated, dirt-cheap flat behind Chance Street – the part of Shoreditch that was, notoriously, 'the leading criminal quarter of all England' in Jack the Ripper's day, and afterwards, England's first council estate, an 1890s Grade II listed council estate, and now in its trendoid incarnation, the only council estate to my knowledge that has a members' bar and a Conran restaurant in it.

The flat may have been a shell with loose wires and ex-posed pipes, it may have had pot holes in the bare concrete floor, it may have had a free-standing toilet that wobbled and occasionally leaked, it may have had a drug-soaked stinky mattress that looked like the Turin Shroud, which I wasted no time in dumping behind the council bins, but it was mine. I was home. Another chance, I hoped . . . some-times London lets down its barrow-boy poker face and is generous like that.

Percolation

Waking up late to the novelty of my new flat, the sounds of London percolating through the walls, blending like the bits between radio stations, the ever-present texture of this city in this third-storey bedroom, floating through a Tuesday morning much like any other . . .

The sounds of the city marinating the block: the imperfect, heavenly practice runs of scales and tune fragments from the classical piano and harp students, those celestial neighbours up on some unspecified floor above, never seen, only imagined, like stories we make up and tell ourselves about heaven, offsetting the hostile vibes from the hooded thugs arguing and boasting round the broken glass and chickenwire of the off-licence, the two-step garage from the bass bins of the drug dealer's car, far-off underwater police sirens, the ever-present racket of the building sites that pepper this area like a patchwork quilt . . . heavenly harp-practice runs offsetting the sounds of sirens, scumbags and construction work, the sounds of London's central drama: advancing money, and the lack of it . . .

Staring out the window as the afternoon fills up with rain, the lines from 'Oranges and Lemons' get stuck on loop in my head . . . 'When will you pay me, say the bells of Old Bailey? When I grow rich, say the bells of Shoreditch' . . . I gaze out of the third-floor window at the grey council block horizon, sipping tea, and I doubt I'll leave the flat all day. Though I'm stranded up here, I'm filled with a strange inner contentment; I don't see the pitbulls outside the Turkish mini-mart, the purse snatchers outside Perfect Fried Chicken; my mind follows the water's flow as it rains across the whole of London, the whole of the Thames Basin stretching out to Oxford, the Cotswolds, the salt marshes of the estuary by my hut; the water in my cup of tea started out the same as this rain, passed through the minerals and rocks of the Thames's table and on into innumerable tributaries, passed through seven other Londoners' bodies before it eventually got to mine. And as I gaze across a gloomy Tuesday afternoon, I open up to a miracle of connectedness: in the rain and the dark waters we are one.

How Much for Two?

D, my musician mate, had just moved into a loft round the corner. D never stayed in one place for long. He'd been in London as long as I had, but he'd lived in twenty-three flats. As a musician, recently he'd become obsessed with the idea of silence. I knew he was getting in deep, and I felt a little concerned when he turned up at the pub with industrial ear shields on – 'the Central Line's so noisy' – and when I asked if he wanted beer, he said no . . . coffee? No . . . tea? 'Just hot water with a bit of lemon', I was a little worried. When he told me he'd given up cigarettes, alcohol and wanking all on the same day last week, it did little to alleviate my concerns . . .

Regardless of his new monastic turn, I presumed he'd somehow lucked out flat-wise, and was expecting an airy, minimalist expanse with tasteful furniture and art, but once I got there I realised his loft was the smelly old attic kind . . . I climbed up the rope ladder through the hole in the roof into a musky, dusty, cave-like space with no windows or natural light . . . I could vaguely make out the mattress of the Spanish drummer he shared the place with through the shadows; my mate's mattress was at the other end of the roof, and to get there you had to crawl under various wooden beams and slats that you kept banging your head really hard on, and then make yourself comfortable amongst the bicycle spokes, dart boards, tennis rackets, broken eighties IBMs and other domestic detritus that had accumulated, out of sight and out of mind, over the last twenty years . . .

The ceiling was too low to stand up straight, and fell off sharply with the angle of the roof, and what with all the beams and slats in the way, we were reduced to crawling around like rats on our hands and knees to get around the place . . . it was one of those freakishly hot days and, being in an attic with no ventilation, it got so sweltering that D stripped down to his undies, and shortly afterwards I did the same, the beads of sweat rolling down my temples as I tried to get comfy on a huge roll of coarse grey carpet underlay . . . I felt like we were the cabin boys on a slave galley from two hundred years ago; after hours of sweating and smoking fags it began to smell like one too, while we huddled round the Apple Mac, seemingly my mate's one possession in the world, and he played me his maddening new loops that that just went round and round like the mind of a man driven insane by years of solitary confinement . . .

By the time we left, I felt like I'd always been in that attic, and I had no idea whether it would be day or night outside, but I got out there and it was pitch black, with a light drizzle in the air . . . we had to make our way into town for a do at the restaurant that first put Soho on the culinary map, when Napoleon's chef set up shop there after Waterloo . . . I realised on the way down I might look a bit out of place in my crinkled shirt and flip flops, but what could I do? The drizzle turned into a torrential downpour and by the time we got there we were soaked . . . I dried off on a luxurious leather sofa underneath a huge oil painting of Edwardian society belles with waiters pouring free flutes of Veuve Clicquot out of silver buckets left, right and centre while I explained to people what a strange day I'd been having and why I was a bit smelly . . . I was plastered in no time at all, trying disastrously to woo a classy American lady with tales of our musical genius . . .

I was beyond repair by closing time and wanted to keep the party going, so when the vaggers of Berwick Street started giving us the eye and hassling us for money I started giving them the eye back and hassling them for drugs . . . we ended up sat in a doorway behind the neon knocking-shop signs with my new friend the crackhead tramp, who passed over his brandy miniature with the bottom knocked off, filled the top up with the flaky white stuff that stood out against his oily soot-black fingers, and let me have a couple of puffs . . .

I breathed out the thick, creamy chemical smoke, feeling sobered up and spacey at the same time, while D got chatting to a snaggletoothed waxy-faced woman. 'How much for two?' he asked, meaning prostitutes; he was always greedy like that, but I suppose if you're going to pay for it you may as well push the boat out . . . '£60, my lovely,' she said . . .

We went over the road to the cashpoint and he got seventy out; I persuaded him to lend me a tenner for a little rock – he could afford it today, his dear old mum had just wired him £100 from back home after he'd pleaded poverty on the phone . . . so we went back and he gave her the money and she told him to wait there . . .

After a couple of minutes it dawned on him that she wasn't coming back; I got my gear off the tramp and we went on a hopeless chase round the warren-like alleys and cuts of Soho . . . I tried to persuade him just to come and have a smoke with me, but the last I saw of him he stormed off swearing he was going to find her and punch her in the face . . .

I walked off laughing to myself, thinking what a clown he was, until I realised I'd been stung too – when I opened up my little goody bag on the bus, the drugs the tramp had given me turned out to be nothing more than a lump of melted bin bag; I wanted to punch him in the face too at first; but as I mulled it over I couldn't help but start laughing again . . . *What a ridiculous day*, I thought . . . London is a trickster's promise that brings you everything and nothing; the streets are paved with fools' gold, and all our stupid hopes and dreams are lit up in neon along them, like carrots to a donkey . . . I chuckled every time I thought about it on that drunken bus ride home . . .

Bicycles

I woke up with a hangover, drooling over a particular hamburger. It was a hamburger from a certain buff, blonde Aussie chain that hits a spot other hangover food cannot reach.

A little later that afternoon I followed the Charing Cross Road on its way down to the Thames, past the Edwardian oyster bar that hid discreetly round the back, down the tall narrow street selling antique maps, Fellini film posters and rare occult books, to the incongruous, trendy burger joint, perched, cuckoo-like, at the end of the row. There were tables outside today, and the gentle dance of light and shade cast by the London plane trees down the thin elegant street lulled me into sitting outside and soaking up the ambience.

The waitress came and took my order.

'Where are you from?' she asked, noticing my stupid accent.
    'The North East,' I said.
    'No, but where exactly?'

'Hartlepool . . .'

'Oh I knew it!' she said, so happy she put her hand on my arm, which was a pleasant surprise. I noticed she had lovely delicate young eyes. She was in London trying to become an actress. People from Hartlepool always had this curiously personal sense of kinship, almost like they were your extended family, in a way only expats from small far-flung towns can. I still feel it too.

'How long have you been in London?' she asked.

'Oh ages, about fifteen years,' I said.

'Wow. You haven't lost your accent. Why did you move to London?' she asked, which I found difficult to put into words . . .

As I tried to formulate an answer, one, two, then a dozen, then hundreds upon hundreds of naked people on bicycles glided past us down the Charing Cross Road . . .

We looked at each other, bemused by this surprise that never seemed to end, that just kept getting more and more surprising, body after naked body on bikes, literally hundreds and hundreds of them – gnarly old naked blokes with snow-white beards, big naked fat blokes with tiny tadgers, naked crusty Spanish birds with dreads and bee-sting tits, hundreds of them gliding down the slope of the Charing Cross Road to the river . . .

'That's why I moved to London!' I giggled.

A Sea

Smoking a cigarette in the small hours, lying next to the skinny suntanned girl, watching her sleeping, her slow breathing, her beauty . . . her long, tanned limbs, that long black thoroughbred hair, like the thick, magnificent mane of the noblest animal I'd ever seen . . .

Waking up to warm morning kisses and the frail early light of an antique rickety room . . . and when it was time to leave her, walking out into a sunny unfamiliar North London like waking up into a dream . . .

That Georgian doorway set back into the wonky terrace that it was so exciting to cross the threshold of the night before . . . piecing together the turn of events and how I ended up there, feeling delighted and bewildered trying to work out how to get to my afternoon appointment, watching North London sleepwalking through its daily affairs, the ding-dong bells of a gilded Georgian clock tower I'd never clapped eyes on before, the dirty yellow London brick the colour of damp sand in the fragile morning sun, London like a city of Georgian sandcastles . . . a neighbourhood I'd not wandered round in years, half-remembered elegant crescents, unfamiliar curves of the canal, London's eternal capacity to appear new and strange, to unexpectedly renew you along with it . . . London still managed to pull off the magic trick way past the seven-year itch – fifteen years in it still had the capacity to feel like 'elsewhere', the charmed enchanted place: unreal streets, dreaming skylines, sunsets over certain crossroads leaving me speechless and still . . .

I got off the bus, crossed the heaving scrum at Leicester Square, a swirling, churning sea of sightseers, followed the slope downwards, riverwards, did a dog-leg into St Martin's Lane, under the awning of the old theatre with the big round light bulbs like the baubles on the trimming of a birthday cake, and instantly I was 21 again, fresh-faced and entranced, in love with London . . . 'I love living in a place like this, where theatre awnings shield you from the drizzle under a glowing line of big round light bulbs,' I once said to myself in a Tuesday afternoon daydream all those years ago . . . I remembered London's exoticness, the feeling of being in a magical other place, back then when it was that to me, when I didn't know where I was going or who I'd find there, and this city was all mystery and promise and future . . . to be young and in love with London: disbelief was suspended, what went up didn't necessarily come down, and London seemed like the great good place where everything was possible . . . and again my heart grew full to bursting, remembering the days when I first fell in love with this city, afternoons drifting into evenings, springtime drifting into Indian summers, those gigantic days when my heart first opened up to this city, and her parks and crescents and countless streets first opened up to me . . .

Lost in these memories, hugging the stately, dream-like elegance of the Garrick Theatre's curve, I wended my way down to the river, as I always seemed to, lost in the folds of the bosom of the metropolis, while the streets of the West End sloped downhill like tributaries to their inevitable end . . .

I found my way across Charing Cross Bridge, to sunset on the South Bank beach, the sun a column of burnished gold leaf across the silvery leaden water . . . a man making a giant sandcastle which would take him long into the evening to finish, an obsession; a weather-beaten man who looked like his wife left him a long time ago and now he was way beyond any of that, just him and his sandcastle and the London sunset . . .

I walked along a dirty tideline, mossy stones, Victorian pottery fragments, an old blackened timber jetty, the squawk of gulls winkle-picking in the wet mud, the smell of muddy sea shore . . . and it struck me: the Thames is a sea, an eternal sea, the sea where little England meets the brave, wide world; Old Father Thames like Old Father Time, our lives here just eddies in its slow, stately flow; and generations of us come and go, searching for this funny kind of life we look for and find in London . . .